CW00820446

About the author

After public school and university, Roderick Archer started his professional life working for a multi-national energy company; this included some spells overseas.

Following this, he worked in the legal department of an engineering company dealing with liability and claims. Later, it led to an invitation to move into a sixth-form college in London, teaching English, law and humanities. He also acquired a passion for writing, for politics and for the City of London, where he is a Freeman of the City.

At present he is teaching English and French while devoting the rest of his time to writing.

Roderick lives in Surrey.

A STRONG WOMAN IN BELGRAVIA: PART ONE

Roderick Archer

A STRONG WOMAN IN BELGRAVIA:
PART ONE

Vanguard Press

VANGUARD PAPERBACK

© Copyright 2021
Roderick Archer

The right of Roderick Archer to be identified as author of
this work has been asserted by him in accordance with the
Copyright, Designs and Patents Act 1988.

All Rights Reserved

No reproduction, copy or transmission of this publication
may be made without written permission.
No paragraph of this publication may be reproduced,
copied or transmitted save with the written permission of the
publisher, or in accordance with the provisions
of the Copyright Act 1956 (as amended).

Any person who commits any unauthorised act in relation to
this publication may be liable to criminal
prosecution and civil claims for damages.

This is a work of fiction. Names, characters, businesses, places,
events and incidents are either the products of the author's
imagination or used in a fictitious manner. Any resemblance to
actual persons, living or dead, or actual events is purely coincidental.

A CIP catalogue record for this title is
available from the British Library.

ISBN 978 1 784659 10 3

Vanguard Press is an imprint of
Pegasus Elliot MacKenzie Publishers Ltd.
www.pegasuspublishers.com

First Published in 2021

Vanguard Press
Sheraton House Castle Park
Cambridge England

Printed & Bound in Great Britain

Dedication

To those who inspire.

BOOK ONE

1

She was in Selfridges doing a spot of shopping. Normally she ordered most of what she needed, but today was different. She was looking for a scarf for one of her friends.

The department store never ceased to amaze her. It was just full of people – customers who were choosing the best. And then there were the staff. As she looked around, she observed a huge number of mainly young female assistants. They were all looking out for customers and all making good use of their interpersonal skills and their knowledge of the quality merchandise.

This was Sable Grantham. Not only was she choosing a scarf, but she also wanted to find a sensible leather wallet for a very special friend. Bloody hell, who's that person over there? she said to herself, as she identified a sheikh followed by several women, all clothed from head to toe in black, with only a slit for their eyes. And who would know they were women, anyway? She wondered if the sheikh was here on holiday. It also crossed her mind that any one of them could be carrying a gun or other dangerous weapon.

Sable was in the store largely because she had been at a loose end that particular afternoon. She had taken a taxi from her home in Belgravia: home was a townhouse in Eaton Place. She just loved fashionable, expensive London. Her full name was Sable Sophie Grantham. She seldom used her full name. Everyone knew her as Sable. She only used her middle name, Sophie, when she was particularly angry or was irritated by someone.

And that was beginning to happen here in this world-famous store. The shop assistant, who wore a black scarf to cover her hair, was searching frantically for both colour and pattern that had been described in detail to her by Sable. She was taking a long time. After consulting her slender watch, Sable looked at a male member of staff, snapped her fingers very audibly and demanded a chair or stool. Soon after she had sat down the female assistant appeared, carrying what she hoped would be suitable goods from which this lady customer could choose.

Sitting on the stool, Sable focused her eyes on the merchandise. She then scanned her eyes over the face of the assistant. The girl was young and had done her make-up quite well. Her eye-shadow was dark, her lips deep red and her skin was obviously well cared for. In terms of attire, the girl wore a black minidress that highlighted good legs under clear tights. Sable had doubted that the girl was wearing stockings. The dark appearance of this girl, who clearly had her origins outside western Europe, gave Sable an idea.

"I think after all I'll choose a black one. Black silk, possibly with small white dots in it," ordered Sable.

Keeping her thoughts to herself, as she had been trained admirably to do, the assistant scurried back into the depths of the drawers to try to locate what Madam had asked for.

Watching all this, from a discreet distance, was the girl's supervisor. She could tell instantly that Madam was giving the girl a hard time. But nevertheless she chose not to interfere, confident that this little Middle Eastern girl would eventually find the correct merchandise that Madam was keen to buy. And so it was that after only a few minutes of searching, the girl proudly presented two scarves to Madam. There were two polka-dot sizes to choose from.

At last Sable was pleased with this girl. Sable chose the small dots, knowing that they would be more versatile and would go well with her boyfriend's dark suits and dark winter coats. The girl was just about to ask Madam if she would like the scarf to be gift-wrapped when Sable swiftly gave orders for it to be done so. As the girl was busy, Sable continued to perch on the stool. She scanned the horizon, taking in the busy customers, browsers and perhaps tourists as well who had just come in for a look at the world-famous store. It was sheer entertainment. For a moment, Sable's eyes met the supervisor's eyes. After a quick appraisal, Sable moved on, taking in the surroundings and the sights and the smells. Make-up or perfume desks were clearly not too far away. Happy with her package, Sable paid with her debit card. As she climbed off the stool she thanked the assistant for her trouble and gave her a quick smile.

After Sable had walked away in the direction of the escalators, the supervisor went to check on her assistant. The girl was mighty pleased that she had eventually made a sale. The supervisor gave her some words of encouragement and a pat on the back for coping with such a difficult woman. The word 'bitch' must have been on their minds, but was never mentioned.

Finding a quiet corner, Sable telephoned home and spoke to her housekeeper, Jane. She told her that she would have a light meal at Selfridges. She also asked if there were any messages. Yes, there was one. A gentleman called Hugh Mannston had telephoned for a friendly chat. Sable smiled.

Hugh Mannston was the prime minister.

2

Sable had chosen a simple meal, mainly quiche, cheese and a salad. To wash it down, she had bought two tumblers of milk. She liked to keep fit and milk gave her strength. Amongst all the diners in the popular cafeteria, Sable was by far the most elegantly dressed. And her make-up was still faultless. Anyone observing her, and that included a man trying to control some fractious children, would have noticed the presence of some Asian blood in her.

Sable was of average height and average build. She had lovely, very slightly dark, oriental features and black hair. Because of its length, she usually wore her hair up. Her legs and thighs were in good shape; she put that down to the large amount of walking that she still liked to do. It was an excellent way to keep fit, she once told Maria, her best friend.

Sable came from mixed parentage. Her father was a solicitor in the City. He worked in the corporate department, dealing mainly with mergers, acquisitions and takeovers. He had stayed with the same firm all his life, having joined straight from school as a sort of apprentice. He had worked for five years as an articled clerk and he had really gained invaluable experience as a youngster. He had worked in several departments during his training, including litigation and commercial conveyancing. It was all part of the job. When he had started working in the corporate department, he worked under the skilful guidance of his principal, a senior solicitor well versed in corporate law. The principal discovered that this young solicitor, Henry Fairfax, had found his métier. Henry was good with detail and he possessed an agile memory. He was also quite good at figures and vocabulary, skills that he had developed at school. They would come in useful when he had to write proposals and suchlike. As Henry proved himself, he was given more and more responsibility. He often worked late, knowing that meeting deadlines was absolutely crucial. He was taught all this by his principal. It was also necessary to meet high standards of professionalism; these were expected by the managing partner.

One day, the principal took Henry along to a business meeting in the City. They were to meet some new clients. This was Henry's reward for his hard work. He would soon discover how negotiations were discussed with a new client representative. Sometimes it was the managing director himself whom they would meet. Clients might be insurance companies, banks, energy companies, shipping lines, pharmaceutical companies, to name but a few. They would state their business objectives. The job of the solicitors' firm was to advise on strategy and how they would achieve that objective. Henry was introduced at the meeting. He was strictly an observer and he was there to learn. He liked what he saw; it all looked manageable to him.

On their way back to the office in the taxi, Henry was asked for his views. "I admire your negotiating style," he said.

The principal let out a small laugh. "Not really. I just tell them what the firm's hourly rate is and then tell them that we can start immediately, even if we can't. It gives them confidence in us," he told Henry. "Confidence and trust – vital."

Back in the office, Henry wondered what his involvement would be. He would be part of a team, he was soon told, examining aspects of finance and taxation. Then there were the banks – merchant banks – supplying essential capital along carefully agreed terms.

Over the next few weeks, Henry was asked to assist on two projects that the department currently had in progress. Sometimes he had to add up lists of figures, check percentages or verify the names of shareholders. He had a good memory, which proved useful at all times. In due course, the firm realised that they had invested in a very useful young solicitor. Henry Fairfax was proving himself at each and every turn.

One day, when he was travelling up in the lifts to his office, he saw an acquaintance with a travel brochure. A company was selling package holidays to Thailand. "An ideal holiday for a bachelor like you. Good value," smiled the stockbroker as he disappeared into the offices on the floor below. Before anyone in the firm was allowed time off for holidays, they had to check with the head of department. Business always came first. It paid their salaries. Henry's boss checked his work sheet and decided that his young, up-and-coming solicitor could take the holiday that he had requested. One major piece of work was behind them. He saw no harm in releasing Henry for his exotic holiday.

"Don't forget to send us a postcard," said the boss with a smile.

3

She was quite short and light and, as far as Henry was concerned, stunningly attractive.

As she lay on top of him, he ran his hands down her back. Her buttocks were like half-moons as he cupped them in his hands. She gave a little laugh. Henry then ran his slim fingers a little deeper until he encountered familiar territory. She was warm and moist. She then moved forward and gave Henry a series of passionate kisses. Henry hoped he had chosen well. After all, this girl had ticked all the right boxes and she was proving to be a little more mature and more sensible than the rest. Also, she spoke English quite well – and that was an added bonus.

As they stood in the shower together, soaping each other down, Henry decided to be bold. He asked her to have dinner with him – and, to his surprise, she said yes. Back at his hotel, Henry chuckled as he stood at the bar with her. She was wearing a lovely dress which accentuated her lovely figure. Her make-up was good and she smiled a lot. He suddenly realised that she was making him happy, and in a serious way.

Over dinner, which was mainly seafood, they talked about London, his job, his home and his wishes for the future. He laughed inwardly when he remembered the postcard that he almost promised to send to his office. How could he tell them that he had met Gloria in a sex parlour in Thailand?

After dinner he escorted her home. In the doorway of her mother's house he gave her a long, passionate kiss and he promised to see her on the following afternoon.

Next morning, after a good sleep, he visited a number of jewellers. After a lot of soul-searching, and thinking, he finally settled on a good quality ring.

That evening, when they were having drinks at their table, he produced the ring box and laid it before her. Gloria looked at the box.

"Er, what is it, please?"

"Gloria, open it, and see if you like it," said Henry. He smiled at her.

Gloria did so and studied the sapphire engagement ring, in wonderment. "Who's it for?" she asked, innocently.

To progress matters, Henry slipped the ring onto her engagement finger and replied happily, "Darling, it's for you. And it fits." She looked at him, unsure whether he was serious or not. Henry was overjoyed. "Darling, I'm asking you to be my wife and spend your life in England with me. I'm a solicitor and I work in the City. Come home with me."

Gloria smiled. "Seriously?"

"Seriously," said Henry.

Then Gloria had a thought. "There's just one thing…"

"What's that?" he asked. He wondered if there was trouble ahead.

"I'll have to ask my mother," she said with a slight smile.

Henry thought for a moment. "No problem. I'll come with you. And after that we'll go and reserve your ticket to London. Oh – do you have a passport?"

She opened her handbag and produced her current passport. "I keep it safe every day."

Henry smiled at her efficiency. "We'll have to go to the British Consulate. You may need a visa. And we'll need to get married."

She looked at him. Her beautiful eyes lit up. He was serious.

***

At the end of his, or rather their holiday, Henry had to travel home to England on his own. Gloria was waiting on her visa. She would then buy her ticket to London Heathrow and join her husband.

Three months later Henry and Gloria were renting a flat in London whilst they went house-hunting. They had to do most of it at weekends because of Henry's heavy workload. He was earning more money. He was also becoming much more knowledgeable now about hostile takeovers and approaches by 'corporate raiders'.

Henry was beginning to become an indispensable part of the team.

Henry's sudden and unexpected marriage, whilst overseas, had completely surprised his boss and the entire team. But when these solicitors met Gloria at the firm's Christmas party, they were stunned by her sheer elegance and beauty. She dressed well. In fact, she put all the partners' wives completely in the shade. Gloria knew how to dress for any occasion. She had been taught this by her mother, and this particular skill would eventually rub off onto her daughter.

4

Henry and Gloria bought a house in south-west London. They set about establishing it as a home as soon as they could. Gloria chose most of the furnishings. The rail link into the City was good. This was most important for Henry who often had to work into the night. Gradually his pay increased as he was given more responsibility. He wondered how long it would take to become a partner.

The next happy event was Gloria's pregnancy. And everyone in the office was thrilled when Henry announced that he was father to a beautiful daughter. It was Gloria who put forward the idea to Henry that they should christen their daughter, Sable. Gloria said she had seen it in a magazine somewhere and it appealed to her. She chose the name Sophie as the middle name, after her mother. Henry was happy to go along with that.

Henry's career flourished in the City. His reputation had by now spread, so much so that he began to receive offers from rival firms. They mostly offered the same thing: a package consisting of a partnership, substantially more money and the car of his choice, plus a seasonticket loan. Henry knew that partners creamed off the profits and made sure that they did quite well. So it was perhaps no surprise when he received an invitation to a partners' meeting. He was informed of his promotion, but also received thanks from the managing partner for declining all the other offers and for not deserting the ship.

"We need you, Henry," he growled.

Henry took the good news home.

"Well," smiled Gloria, "I have a partner who's now a partner. That can't be bad." Henry gave her a lovable kiss and squeezed her bottom. "You can tell me about it in bed," she said.

He then told Gloria that it was now time to think seriously about a private school for Sable, who was growing up fast. There was Millfield in Somerset, well known for sports and equestrianism, but Henry favoured something else. Together, he and Gloria settled on a good London day school. It seemed sensible.

And so it was that against this background of stability, and respectability, that Sable Fairfax grew up. She did well enough at school. She was not particularly academic, but she knew enough to do all her homework, read good books and make friends. It was in the latter area where she did well. She also discovered that she had a leaning towards modern languages; she also did quite well in Latin, which greatly pleased her father, being a solicitor.

After achieving good grades in both French and German, she decided to read Modern Languages at

London University. Both her parents thought it was an excellent choice, and wise to concentrate on her strengths. Her friends from school were quick to realise that Sable Fairfax had inherited her mother's good looks, and probably her father's brain. She had plenty of girlfriends, mainly from school, and just a few eager male admirers.

Her mother made sure that Sable would have an all-round education. Whilst her daughter enjoyed bookwork, learning grammar and conversing in either French or German with her friends, her mother took her to art galleries. This was after Gloria had realised that her lovely daughter showed little interest in museums, apart from London's Victoria and Albert.

Sable found the National Gallery and the National Portrait Gallery to be absolutely fascinating. She was stunned at the vastness of the National Gallery and loved the paintings. Not only had she discovered a likeness for Rubens, but she was fascinated by the interpretations of the various artists. A friend later told them that there were excellent collections of art to be seen at the Wallace Collection in Manchester Square. Apsley House was also worth an in-depth visit, so she was told. Art brought the world alive to Sable, whereas pottery and stone just left her cold – stone cold.

When she was leaving the National Gallery one afternoon with her friend, they stood there overlooking Trafalgar Square.

"What's that street in the distance? " she asked.

Her friend looked. "Oh, that's Whitehall. It leads to Downing Street, amongst other places – where the prime minister lives."

Sable was thinking. "Oh really." However, a plan began crystallising in her mind.

They then turned and gazed at all the tourists, milling about, entertained by the performers. The tourists consisted mostly of orientals: Chinese, Japanese, Koreans and such like; the Europeans were in a minority. She and her friend, Maria, whom she had met at school, went to have tea and a scone at the nearby teahouse.

"Darling, remind me, who's the prime minister these days?" Sable asked quite innocently.

Maria looked at her and smiled. "Still the same woman in charge. Don't you remember, she took over after that chap suddenly resigned? It was all a bit of a bomb-shell. It must have taken the Queen by surprise. It took the country by surprise."

"The Queen?" said Sable, slightly perplexed. She suddenly realised that she had to brush up on news, current affairs and government. There were gaps in that part of her education.

Maria continued, "Darling, she's head of our Constitution, but is strictly non-political. She has to agree to new Acts of Parliament for final sign-off. The prime minister has a weekly audience with the monarch as well."

Sable stared, in awe, at her friend's knowledge. She was then emphatic. "Languages are my strength. I converse well in French." She then chuckled, "There's nothing quite like a good French letter!"

The two girls howled with laughter, much to the intense amusement of the other customers, some of whom stared at them.

"Totally protective?" asked Maria.

"Well, isn't that the whole point," added Sable, with a naughty giggle.

Maria's knowledge of British history and the British Constitution was impressive, her knowledge of languages less so. Whereas with Sable, it was the other way round. Hence her need to brush up on British politics and learn about some of the other western European leaders.

"When will we next have a male prime minister?" asked Sable, in all simple curiosity.

Maria thought for a minute. "Yes. Good question. It depends on a number of factors, such as the timing of the next general election and who enjoys the confidence of their political party as leader." Sable nodded. She was beginning to learn a thing or two from Maria.

Maria then asked her about her university course. She knew that Sable would have to go abroad fairly soon.

"I'll be spending several months in Paris and then several months in Berlin. I'm really looking forward to it," said Sable with some intensity.

"Is Daddy footing the bill?" asked Maria cheekily, knowing full well that he would be.

Sable nodded. "Yes." She looked around. "The grant does not really cover things like that. But I'll be in a good position to pick up some informal aspects of both languages, and how they live."

"Learning local colloquialisms will be invaluable," observed Maria, "and you'll be a much sought-after person when you return – and indeed when you complete your course."

"I'll have to learn a bit about French politics," added Sable.

The two girls chatted on, during which time Sable discovered that the role of the French prime minister was below that of the French president. Maria recalled from her textbook knowledge that after a nationwide election, the president appoints a prime minister. The PM always comes from the party that controls the chamber. The prime minister serves as head of government and is in charge of domestic policy and day-to-day governing. He also recommends, for presidential approval, the other members of the cabinet. The French president has been made more powerful as compared to the prime minister. Sable was listening as Maria continued, "The Prime Minister is the executor of laws as passed by the parliament and signed by the president."

"You seldom hear of him on national news," declared Sable. Maria suggested to Sable that she read various newspapers, magazines or even the French press, via the internet. She could always buy Paris Match.

Sable nodded. Perhaps she would discover more about these politicians when she was in Paris.

5

Sable took Maria back home to have supper with her parents. Henry was still at work; this time he was involved in a heavy takeover battle. "He's been working long hours almost every day," complained Gloria. "Anyway, he told us to make a start."

Gloria had produced a light curry which she thought they would all enjoy. They were not in their lovely dining room, with its long polished mahogany table. Instead, they sat at the table in the conservatory. Gloria was at the head, with the two girls at each flank, so that they could face each other.

Gloria fully approved of Maria as best friend to her daughter. Over the years, ever since they had met at school, Maria had had a calming influence on Sable. She had even managed to get Sable out of a few scrapes, one of which almost involved the Police. Sable was once on the threshold of taking the law into her own hands. She had been out in a pub. For some reason she did not like the way she had been served a drink: there was too much ice. In fact, as she recollected, she had asked for the drink with no ice, but the barmaid had almost insisted, much to the considerable annoyance of Sable. She was on the point of throwing the glass, complete with ice, back into the barmaid's face. And if a barman or manager got in the way – tough! Luckily, Maria, who had just returned from the ladies, gasped and ran forward. She caught hold of the glass, and pulled Sable back onto the chair where she had been sitting.

"I'm so sorry. She can get agitated," said Maria, as she threw the apology over her shoulder and calmed Sable at the same time. Once they were outside, Maria told Sable to calm down and behave herself. She tried to convince Sable that barmaids can sometimes make simple mistakes. "Darling, they are usually trained how to serve drinks – you know, a slice of lemon, here and there."

Sable was still angry, rather like a spoilt child. "A slice of lemon would have been better than all that silly ice! Who needs it?"

Maria studied her. "If you had thrown it, I think they might have been justified in calling the police."

"For what?" argued Sable, still moody.

"Assault," replied Maria. "You were so close!"

As Maria recalled these events, Gloria offered the girls more fruit juice and water from the glass carafe on the table.

The mild curry was a great success. "I used to make it in Thailand. Mother loved it," she beamed. Gloria then went on to tell Maria how much she had loved cooking; it was one of her other part-time occupations, when she was not attending to the somewhat intimate needs of her part-time customers. She described that part of her life as 'hostessing', which covered a whole manner of things, and often a multitude of sins.

They had all loved the meal. Part of it had been left over for Henry, who could come in at any time. He just loved curry, too. It reminded him of a special meal once in Bangkok. It was over cheese and celery that Sable talked about her university course and how much she liked it. She then told them the funny story of how a friend had brought them some cheese back from France. The friend had been shocked to discover that the very same cheese was on sale in the larger English supermarkets at a considerably reduced price.

"Market economics, I suppose," commented Maria. Gloria nodded her agreement.

Good news. It was then that Henry walked in. Gloria rushed to the door and threw her arms around her husband and gave him a warm and loving kiss. It was pure passion.

Maria watched in awe, wondering if she would ever feel the same about a husband one day – whenever that day should come. It was so very delightful to see pure sexual chemistry, between husband and wife, and still very much alive.

After a wash, Henry came and sat down. He began to devour the plate in front of him. Gloria sat smiling. Maria glanced at them all, and then, when she thought the time was right to ask a question, she did so.

"How's the City, Henry?"

Henry sat there, eating away. Then he replied, "Everybody's got the urge to merge… It's silly." Sable sat there, admiring her clever father pronounce judgement. He continued, "But it's the hostile takeovers and corporate acquisitions that I like. Then there's the City Takeover Panel to always consider: their work is important." He turned to face Maria. "I like to be busy. And, yes, I like responsibility."

Gloria butted in, "He's never happier than when he's working flat out." The two girls smiled at Gloria. But it was Maria who wondered how well the marriage was surviving under this intense workload. And it was as if Gloria had been reading her thoughts.

She was suddenly very candid. "We reserve Saturday and Sunday nights for our passion." She then lowered her voice a little. "And it's still most exciting."

Henry caught the end of their conversation and smiled lovingly at his still-gorgeous wife. "My darling, you always were good at keeping on top of things – especially in the bedroom."

Sable giggled at her parents as Maria was still putting two and two together. Sable realised that Henry and Gloria were probably still very good performers and she suspected that it was her mother who took the initiative, partly based on her former professional life in Bangkok.

"Have some more cheese, Maria," suggested Gloria, "It's Somerset's best."

Maria declined. "Gosh, thank you, no. It was lovely – nice and mature. But I really ought to get along." Maria thanked Gloria for the lovely supper, wished Henry a pleasant evening and then went to collect her coat. Sable went with her. The two girls stood by the front door, chatting. Maria knew that Sable would be going to Paris soon to learn her French; Maria wondered if she would have a chance to visit her.

"You'll probably have a fantastic social life," commented Maria.

Sable became more serious when she said that her college in London had allowed her to take her course at the Sorbonne, and they expected great things of her. She talked about regular reports being sent to London.

"Now that is serious," said Maria. "But I'm sure you will do just fine."

They said their goodbyes and parted.

As Maria took her bus home, she just could not put the image of Henry and Gloria making love out of her mind. But she had to admit it made her giggle when she realised who was on top.

6

Sable soon found herself in Paris. She was that sort of person. She had a room in college buildings which was adequate and she could walk to the Sorbonne. That suited her well. She knew she would have to study plenty of French literature, so a disciplined approach was needed. That was what Henry had insisted upon.

The classrooms and lecture rooms had all been modernised and even the library, where she would find most of her books, was not exactly the stuffy place that she had imagined. Even one of the boys on the reception desk was quite good-looking. Most of the teaching staff were women; one or two of them were quite severe. One professor, in particular, was very short and always looked nervous, almost like a very frightened rabbit. It was hard to know when to approach her for advice. But in terms of their academic ability, they knew their books and how to teach.

Sable had plenty of homework, too. Her ability to write correct French, and use perfect grammar, was important in her written answers. She had classes in business French, which particularly impressed Henry. And it was here that she also had to do a lot of speaking, sometimes in front of the class. She would also have to answer questions from her classmates, some of which were quite exacting. And then there were class discussions, which sometimes provoked passionate outbursts from some of the other foreign students.

It was in the student refectory that Sable started to become acquainted with some of her peers. And they, in turn, were happy to introduce her to some of their friends. It was suggested that they could meet in one of the popular student haunts after supper.

Sable tried to keep to her regular habit of doing homework immediately after classes. That way she kept on top of things. She was quite well disciplined when it came to work and it usually paid off. She was being rewarded with promising grades by most of her professors. This was the sort of news that her parents were expecting.

***

"I'm Henri. So good to meet you."

Sable guessed that the young man, with whom she was shaking hands, was a trifle younger than her. He had a fresh face and fair hair. He was slim and athletic. Having been addressed in English, she decided to respond in English. "My name is Sable," she said with a broad smile. "I know, it's French for sand – funny, n'est-ce pas?"

Henri looked at her, up and down. "Please be careful, and don't get blown away," he said with a friendly smile.

"I assure you there's no chance of that. Actually, sable is also an adjective, meaning black or gloomy, but I'm far from gloomy," she replied.

"May I buy you a drink – something soft, perhaps?"

Sable settled on an orange juice and sat down on a nearby stool. They were in a student bar not far from the college. It was time to relax for a while. She had done her homework and felt she was entitled to meet some new faces. One of her girlfriends came to say hello and chat about work. Sable was curious to learn more about Henri – she wondered if anyone knew him. When she pointed out that it was Henri who was buying her a drink, her friend was quick to point something out to her.

"He's the son of the French prime minister, Roland Tassier."

"Oh my goodness!" exclaimed Sable. "But how very interesting, nevertheless. Perhaps I can learn a thing or two about French politics."

The two girls sat and chatted while they waited for Henri to return. He came back, laden with three glasses: the spare was for Sable's friend. Thoughtful. After Henri had chatted to them both about generalities, Sable thought it was time to ask a few questions. She asked him about his course.

"Well, I think I'm improving my knowledge of English. I'm certainly improving my knowledge of history, literature and politics," he said with a boyish grin.

"And I gather your father is in politics in a big way?" she asked.

Henri looked at both girls, uncertain how much they knew. "Dad's doing all right," he smiled.

It was Sable who was dying to correct his English. "Your father is running much of the country, while the president runs the other half, helps formulate foreign policy and is the 'face' of France." She paused for a moment. "I would very much like to meet Monsieur Tassier before my course is over," she said eloquently. She smiled at him, willing him to extend an invitation.

Henri paused to think, then drank some beer. "I'm sure something can be arranged," he said in a positive tone. "By the way, what does your father do, if you don't mind me asking?"

After complimenting him on his excellent English, she told Henri that her father was a solicitor, or advocate, as they say on the continent. She told him he worked in offices in the City, the oldest administrative borough of local government, right in the heart of London.

Henri was impressed. He told Sable that he had visited London as a tourist once and liked what he saw. It was grand and huge. She in turn informed him that if he wanted to pursue a course in London, then the

London School of Economics and Political Science might be the place for him, especially if he wanted to follow in his father's footsteps into politics. Henri nodded, saying that he knew the place all right. Perhaps he ought to discuss the matter when his father had a free moment.

***

When Sable next phoned home, she told her mother that she was making good progress. And yes, she would put her grades in the next post. Gloria was particularly interested to hear about her daughter meeting the son of the French prime minister – and almost with the same Christian name. She went on to say that Henry was doing some private work for, yes, our own prime minister. Gloria simply said it was something 'legal', and didn't know the ins and outs of it. But it would look incredibly good on his CV.

Sable was so happy for her hard-working father; she sent her love and said she would try to come home by train on the next long weekend. Meanwhile she said she hoped to see Henri again, socially. Also, she wanted to learn more about his father and the 'office of prime minister' in France.

On her next free afternoon, Sable took a bus into the seventh arrondissement, central Paris. Using her guidebook, she soon found the Rue de Varenne. She walked slowly, admiring the buildings. They were in good condition, given their age, and had not suffered damage in the Second World War, neither in 1940 nor in 1944. She walked on and located number fifty-seven. This, the Hotel Matignon, was the official residence of the prime minister of France. Sable was impressed by the baroque architecture, the building having been completed in 1725. Its rich interiors made the building one of the most elegant and most frequented mansions in Paris.

She read from her guidebook: the prime minister of France occupies an important position in the French constitutional system. He or she takes a leading part in the working of the French government. Executive powers are shared between the president and the prime minister; the latter is the executor of laws as passed by Parliament and signed by the President. The president is the elected leader of France and the prime minister is the nominee of the president.

And so Sable now had a much better appreciation of what role Roland Tassier played in the French government. As she stood there and admired the building, she wondered if Henri could at least spirit her in through the back door. All he had to do was get her past the armed policemen! Equipped with this knowledge, Sable would now be in a better position to talk to Henri, her new friend. She could at least now ask him if he enjoyed his weekends at Hotel Matignon.

During the next week Sable really applied herself at the Sorbonne and was rewarded with some high grades. She looked forward to telling her mother. She saw Henri once or twice and proudly informed him that she had seen 'the mansion' in the Rue de Varenne.

"You should have told me," he said defensively.

"Well, I was a tourist, and not properly dressed to come in," she replied, almost by way of an apology. "I'm going back home next weekend – need to see my parents."

Henri smiled. "When you return, we must make that appointment. I'll speak to my mother."

"That would be nice."

7

By the end of the week, Sable was on the train back to London. She sat there thinking about Henri. She found him young yet sexually attractive. She wondered what his father was like – she knew he was also quite young.

Roland Tassier was a very young prime minister, possibly one of the youngest that France had ever had. He was barely forty. Sable had read that he wanted to rebuild the country, repair the economy by reducing unemployment and putting quotas on immigration. Sable sighed. Would it really work, she asked herself. These were noble ambitions – but. She would ask her mother when they had a chance to chat. Gloria loved questions on politics.

And so the train continued on its swift journey to London. Once there, in its northern terminal, Sable made her way to Waterloo on the Underground. After changing trains again, she was soon home. Her mother welcomed her home and immediately started asking about 'school reports' as she put it. This was always a bit of a bore for Sable but she co-operated with her strict mother, gave her some papers and was duly rewarded with a glass of champagne.

Gloria looked at the paperwork. "Darling, you are doing very well. Now tell me about this student friend of yours, Henri."

"He's the son of the prime minister and he lives in the Hotel Matignon – such opulence, I tell you. Baroque style."

"And his mother?" asked Gloria. Sable was unsure because she had not yet had the invitation to the magnificent mansion – but she assumed Henri's mother also lived there. Gloria was insistent. She put great store in developing social contacts at all levels as soon as possible, especially if overseas in an attractive country. And Paris qualified admirably, and Gloria just longed to make a visit.

She then wondered if Henry could influence his firm to open a Paris office. Surely, all he had to do was convince the other partners that there was good corporate business on the other side of the Channel. And how many French companies or banks were there in London?

"Darling, secure an invitation to the Hotel Matignon as quickly as possible. Manipulate little Henri. A smile can open so many doors."

Sable, who had suddenly been rather glum, realised her potential and that what her clever mother was advising was sheer common sense. As soon as she next saw him, she would smile warmly and put the invitation at the forefront of his mind. Henri's mother was bound to arrange something for this charming undergraduate from England. After all, she and Henri might just strike up a close friendship.

When they had time to chat, her father took in all the rest of the detail. He firmly supported Gloria. The sooner she got to know the boy's parents, the better it would be.

"Perhaps his father will give you a tour of the house – smile, and be pushy. It's the only way to get on," her father had said. "He's bound to do quite a lot of official entertaining as well," he added.

Sable had some letters to deal with, one of which was from her university asking her about accommodation in Berlin. It was wise to reserve a place well in advance. Sable filled out the form and showed it to her mother before posting it. Her mother had also wisely suggested that she buy a small present for Henri, such as aftershave or chocolates. "Try and give them to him as soon as you can; that might just hasten things," said Gloria.

Her long weekend soon came to an end; in no time at all the express train was hurtling towards northern Paris. Sable was looking forward to her final few weeks and also some examinations. She received a message at the Sorbonne. She was intrigued to discover that it was an invitation to the Hotel Matignon the following Friday afternoon. Sable telephoned home to tell her mother immediately.

"Right, darling, deliver your present to Henri as soon as you can. Next week, put on a nice dress and put your hair up." Sable knew that these were orders to be obeyed. Sable was used to dressing up. She looked forward to this visit to the seat of power enormously. She just hoped the week would pass quickly. Henry and Gloria had told her to expect afternoon tea.

When Sable saw Henri at lectures, she handed over the present. He was overjoyed and thanked her graciously. He also asked her not to be late for the function. Sable made him a promise.

The days passed quickly and suddenly it was Friday. As Sable approached the fine building she reminded herself that it had been completed long before the French Revolution. In the sumptuous courtyard there were black limousines all lined up on either side. Sable assumed that they belonged to politicians – and what a wonderful way to travel. She just hoped that they all deserved it.

Before she could proceed any further, she was quite suddenly met by a member of the household staff. The gentleman, who wore a uniform almost equivalent to morning clothes, gently ushered her to the entrance. He explained, in faultless English, that she would be received by the French prime minister and would, in due course, meet Henri.

As Sable turned and almost stared again at the expensive limousines, the usher spoke to her. He almost read her mind. "Mademoiselle Fairfax, you have arrived at an interesting event, a social event, held on Fridays. Some politicians, and also a few diplomats, are here today. May I advise you of the protocol: the house usher will ask you for your name and it will then be called out as you are about to be received by the prime minister of France – Monsieur Tassier." Sable stared at him, in awe. "Mademoiselle Fairfax, do you have any questions?"

Sable just shook her head. "Thank you. No." She forced a smile. "Merci." Thus, Sable made history in the Fairfax family by entering the 'hallowed portals,' as she later referred to them, of the Court of the French prime minister.

Speaking excellent French was no problem. But she felt so nervous. However, as it turned out, both the PM and the lady beside him put her at her ease by smiling happily at her and talking in easy French. The lady introduced herself simply as Brigitte. She told Sable that Henri was on the other side of the room and was waiting for her. Sable did a very quick curtsey in front of Brigitte before turning, only to be confronted by a waitress laden with champagne. Sable took a glass and then set about weaving her way in and out of tall gentlemen in dark suits, as she searched for Henri.

He came across and found her. "Hello, Sable. Cheers. Glad you made it."

"Cheers." She raised her glass, thankful that they had finally found each other.

He explained that his parents wanted to treat her to a special afternoon since her time in Paris was limited.

"But how kind of them," she said, as her eyes wandered all around the room, taking in various ladies and gentlemen.

Henri also scanned the room. "The Dutch prime minister is also here, plus a few other dignitaries. Would you like to meet him?" Before she could think of any kind of mild protest, Henri was escorting her in the general direction of a group of gentlemen, one of whom was the Dutch PM. She was amazed at how relaxed and confident Henri was.

The Dutch PM recognised Henri immediately. And as his penetrating blue eyes settled on Sable, he extended his hand graciously. "Schmidt, Gerit Schmidt, Mademoiselle; delighted to make your acquaintance," he said with a broad smile. He had a clear complexion and black hair and was of medium height.

"Enchanté," replied Sable. "I, too, am very pleased to meet you, sir."

The Dutch PM looked at Sable, admiring her good looks, a bit like a trainer inspects a new racehorse. He also smiled at Henri and this prompted a question. "Are you two together? Henri, tell me, where did you discover this charming lady?"

Before Henri could reply, Sable was quick to put things straight. "Mr Schmidt, we are both students at the Sorbonne. I'm from London. When I finish my course, I shall be moving on to Berlin to brush up and improve my German."

"Ah," said Gerit Schmidt jovially, "such a wonderful English expression: to 'brush up'. Not to be confused with sweeping floors!" They all laughed heartily at the Dutchman's joke. Still smiling, the Dutchman looked at Henri. "And tell me, Henri, what are your plans? Are you going to follow this lovely English lady to Berlin?"

Henri smiled, almost started to speak, but was cut off by Sable who rescued a slightly awkward situation.

"Mr Schmidt, my father is a solicitor in London, in what we call the 'City' – the very old part near the Royal Exchange, Bank of England and Tower of London."

" Ah, that very old part, built by the French when you became a colony of France."

Sable thought quickly. "Well, of Normandy, actually."

Gerit Schmidt corrected himself. "Of course."

Suddenly two junior diplomats descended upon the Dutch PM and whisked him away to another part of the room. Gerit barely had time to throw a 'goodbye' over his shoulder as he left the two young ones to talk to each other.

"That was fun, and unusual," commented Sable.

It was then that Brigitte at last found time to come over and talk to her son and his English friend. She apologised for staying away for so long. She put it down to pressure of work.

"Affairs of State," she murmured. "Some of them just get passed from one minister to the next, with nobody bothering to resolve the issue. It's really not good enough."

"Politicians always inherit problems, especially when someone's term is ending," commented Henri. "Anyway, we spoke to the Dutch PM."

Brigitte examined him. "Very good. Well done, darling." Brigitte nodded her head, acknowledging that unresolved issues can sometimes mount up. "In about thirty minutes time we will go into that room for a buffet supper. Roland will join us," said Brigitte in a hopeful tone.

8

They had adjourned to another room in the delightful Hotel Matignon. It was only used for entertaining, so Henri was not well acquainted with the paintings on the walls, nor the grand clocks. He and Sable examined one of the clocks that stood on a marble pedestal. It read 'Boucheret à Paris'. They noted the time was accurate, which pleased them.

After they had been introduced, the French prime minister enjoyed a conversation with Sable. They talked about her course, her friendship with Henri, her parents back in London and how often she might return to Paris. When pressed about her possible future career, she said it was much too early to lay any definite plans. She added that her languages might take her into the Civil Service or the Foreign Office. She would probably not go into the law as her father had done. Roland Tassier seemed convinced and impressed that this girl knew what she wanted. As for Henri, Roland said that he and Brigitte had discussed some options but he really needed to complete his course first, with good grades. Sable liked Henri's parents. They were young, good looking and very positive.

When the evening was over it was clear that Henri's parents had greatly enjoyed their meeting with Sable. They concluded that she was, at least for the time being, a suitable friend for Henri.

Sable thanked her host and hostess for a truly lovely time. Henri was asked to escort her to one of the cars that would act as a taxi ride home. They gave the address to the driver. No problem. He knew Paris very well, even the seedier districts. He had passed his taxi exams long ago.

When they arrived at her lodgings, she got out and thanked the driver. She told him how much she had enjoyed meeting the prime minister and Madame Tassier.

The driver was slightly puzzled. "Do you mean the lady called Brigitte?"

Sable smiled. "Yes."

The driver then thought about it. "It is probably okay for me to say this but you have Monsieur Tassier, for sure, but the lady has another name: she is Mademoiselle Brigitte —" He then used another surname. It slightly took Sable's breath away. She thanked the driver and off he went, back to the wonderful mansion.

Once home, Sable immediately searched the internet. Sure enough, she found her answer. It was time to make a phone call.

***

Gloria was overjoyed to hear all this news, especially the mixing and mingling with other prime ministers. What next?

Henry then took the phone. "What was Matignon like?" Sable described the interior, the chandeliers, the clocks and all the staff in their livery or uniforms. She said she had been treated like royalty.

"And the son, Henri?"

She said he had been a very polite host and friend, looking after her at all times.

"Well done, darling. Come home when your course is over."

He gave the phone back to Gloria to carry on chatting. Thank goodness the phone call was free.

When it was all over, Gloria sat with Henry at the kitchen table. She was suddenly very serious.

"Well," said Henry, "what did you discover?"

"Her name is Brigitte Pousson, Mademoiselle Pousson," said Gloria.

Henry stifled a schoolboy laugh. "What? Well, that makes poor Henri —"

"Exactly," commented Gloria. "Poor little chap. Why don't they get married?"

"Who? Sable and Henri? " exclaimed Henry.

"No! This chap Tassier and girlfriend Pousson. They should have done it years ago." She looked at her husband. Henry sat there, contemplating. Was Roland Tassier against marriage? Was he one of those free liberal thinkers? Was she against marriage? What was their reason? And did they need a reason if they were fully committed to each other?

"Tell me, darling," asked Gloria, "do heads of state have to be married, or senior politicians and whatnot?"

Henry recalled some facts. "Mr Heath was a bachelor and became prime minister. And I think France had a president who was also unmarried."

Sable had told her mother that the Dutch PM was good-looking and had been very attentive when Henri had introduced Sable to him.

"I'm glad she has met him but she really has got to maintain her focus on her course. Boyfriends can wait. Don't you agree, darling?" Gloria looked at Henry for support.

Henry agreed that his daughter must concentrate on her exams. As soon as she was home, she would be packing her bags for Berlin.

"How long will she have in London?" asked Henry.

"About a week, I think."

***

Sable wrote her letters of thanks to the French prime minister and to Brigitte, and to Henri for being such a good friend and guide. The prime minister's residence was something to be seen, for sure. She had been quick to point out that the British prime minister also lived in a government building.

When she next saw Henri it was during her last few days at the Sorbonne. They had been to some final seminars together as the exams concluded. A farewell party had been arranged for the students. It proved to be quite emotional for some of the girls as they had formed, what they hoped would be, lifelong friendships.

As Sable chatted to Henri, she couldn't help also thinking about Gerit Schmidt. He had a lovely smile and he had looked at her in a certain way. She wondered when she might see him again. He was obviously a career politician.

At the end of the party, Henri escorted Sable back to her rooms. "I hope we can keep in touch, Sable. It's been a wonderful few months. I hope your next course is just as successful."

Sable gave him a quick kiss. "I'll write to you from Berlin. Will you still be at the Hotel Matignon?" He said they would, so long as the president remained the same. She gave him a quick hug and thanked him for simply everything.

"Let's stay friends forever," he said with a boyish grin.

Sable thanked him, went in and closed the door.

As she put together some last-minute packing, she set her alarm clock for her early morning walk to the taxi rank. From there, it was a short ride to the railway station. As she lay in bed she thought about Henri. He was such a nice young chap but young for his age. She also liked his father, Roland. For a prime minister, he too was very young and also very attractive.

Next morning found Sable on the train heading north, out of France and back to England. She sat there with her thoughts. It had been a successful course at the Sorbonne. Her business French was much improved and, thanks to becoming a Parisian resident, albeit for a few months, her knowledge of colloquial French was much improved. She had made some new friendships, at various levels, and she had even penetrated the portals of the residency of the prime minister. Such activity was not normally part of the curriculum.

Once back in London, she changed trains. On the suburban service out of Waterloo, Sable found herself sitting opposite a dark-skinned woman, probably from the West Indies. The woman wore a very tight miniskirt and very obvious red panties. At a train stop she happened to drop her passport. It was clear that she was from Jamaica. Sable identified the woman as a bit of tart, popularly known as a red 'jam tart'.

Once she was back home it would be time to start her revision work on her German language. She knew that her accent was good but she needed to expand her vocabulary.

Her parents greeted her home. It was Friday night and Henry had especially come home in time for dinner with his 'two girls'. Over dinner they chatted about all that she had seen and done, especially socially. But it was Henry who wanted to know how Sable thought she had done, since French was the stronger of her two foreign languages.

"I feel confident that I'll find my final year in London so much easier, and all the better for going to foreign universities," said Sable with confidence.

"Excellent," said Henry. "But do apply yourself at least as hard, if not harder, in Berlin. Don't forget, academic work always comes first. Berlin bars come second."

"We've already had the first call for fees," Gloria mentioned.

Sable promised both her parents that she would be a diligent student in Berlin. Henry hoped that German discipline would also rub off onto her and would keep her focused on her course.

They went out to dinner on Saturday night. This was preceded by them enjoying a bottle of champagne at home. Gloria insisted that they have just one glass each before going out; the rest they could have upon their return.

"Don't forget, darling, the Germans are great beer and lager drinkers," advised Henry with caution. He watched Sable tuck into her lobster. "Best to be on your guard. I'm sure it's quite easy to go to some bars and drink all night and into the dawn."

"Darling, our daughter will never do such things," said Gloria with emphasis. Gloria smiled at them both. She could see that her daughter had matured through her time in France. She did her best to convince Henry that Sable would be sensible.

Henry turned to his side and held his wife's hand and then gave her a kiss. As he did so he admired her beauty and the lovely black dress that she had chosen to wear. She looked stunning, as always. He patted her little bottom. The sexual chemistry between Henry and his wife was still very much alive. She went to great efforts to always please him in bed, often lying on top of him while they enjoyed superb passion. Sometimes they even managed it mid-week. And Henry was also skilful at pleasing Gloria's physical needs.

Sunday was to be a relaxing day. Everyone got up late and breakfasted as they wished. Henry and Gloria got on with various domestic chores while Sable took her mother's advice and started choosing things that she would need in Germany, especially in the cold winter months.

"They usually have snow, darling, so pack some boots," Gloria advised as she called up the stairs, "and a scarf."

On Tuesday the postman's bundle happened to contain two letters for Sable. One of the letters was from the university and contained joining instructions for the language school in Berlin, and general advice for air travellers. The other letter, which also looked official, had come from the Dutch embassy in London.

Sable opened it in her bedroom. To her intense surprise it was from Gerit Schmidt. He said he had remembered Sable from her time in Paris at the Hotel Matignon. He was in London on business and could he meet her socially? Inside the letter there was an invitation to a drinks reception at the embassy. Gerit hoped to see her there.

Goodness, she thought. She opened her diary quickly and realised that she just had a few days before departing.

She telephoned the number at the embassy, spoke to someone and said she would be pleased to attend the reception.

"The Dutch prime minister! Good Lord. Well, you had better go, and maintain good Anglo-Dutch relations," said her father in an encouraging tone.

"I met him briefly in Paris, with Henri at my side," added Sable.

Henry looked at Gloria. "What do you think, darling?"

"I would say, never turn down an invitation – you never know what might flow from it." Then Gloria looked at Sable. "Is he nice? I mean, he is the PM."

Sable was at a slight loss for words. "He seemed very pleasant. I suppose I'll find out."

***

Sable made her way to the Dutch embassy partly by Underground and partly by bus. Her father always liked buses. Arriving close to the venue in SW7, Sable walked to the address at Hyde Park Gate. There was some evidence of limousines outside but not quite like the presence that she had seen outside the Hotel Matignon.

The main door was open and Sable showed her invitation card to the hall staff. In front of her was a small queue of guests, all undergoing a rigorous security check. It appeared that everything metallic had to be deposited in a box before being pushed through an X-ray machine. This would include rings, keys and wristwatches. Sable stared at the man in front – he had even removed his braces. She just hoped his trousers would not suddenly fall down! Sable removed her light jewellery and keys and then she was shown through the metal arch. It was just like airport security.

She followed the line of guests forward and soon saw that all the guests were being received. The lady in front of her turned round and whispered that it was a lady ambassador, plus her husband and someone else. Sable wondered what the protocol was on greeting an ambassador. She prepared for a brief exchange of words, remembered the words 'Your Excellency' and a very fast little curtsey. Even if no one else performed the latter, it would look good.

Suddenly it was over, when a member of the embassy staff approached her. "Miss Fairfax?"

Sable turned and smiled. "Yes."

"Would you come with me, please?"

Before she could utter another word, Sable was given a glass of champagne. She was then ushered towards a tall, slim gentleman who temporarily had his back to her. His aide rotated him quickly so that Sable suddenly came face to face with Gerit Schmidt, the Dutch PM and sender of her invitation.

The grin was familiar. "Sable – how good that you could come. Delighted to see you again." Gerit gave her a kiss on both cheeks and raised his glass. "Cheers. Now tell me, did you enjoy Paris?"

As Sable described the course that she had just completed at the Sorbonne, she was aware of Gerit's penetrating blue eyes. He seemed to be examining her body and form as she was speaking. It was a bit unsettling. This was something to add to her email to Maria: she might ask her for some advice. "And I made a good friend in Henri Tassier," she added.

"Of course. I, too, have great affection for Roland and Brigitte. They are a nice couple. Tell me, when do you leave for Berlin?"

"At the end of the week."

Gerit thought for a moment. "Clearly, I must visit the German Chancellor as often as possible, and see you at the same time." In her naiveté, Sable wondered if the Dutch prime minister could do such things.

The attractive lady ambassador then came up to have a few words with Gerit, who quickly apologised to Sable as he broke away. It was almost an honour to be admired by a senior politician: Gerit clearly liked her.

But then she recalled that, in spite of his youth, she realised that she would always have a lot of time for Henri. It was safe territory.

Unsure where to go next, she gingerly moved over to a group. She discovered that they were embassy staff. A tall pleasant man introduced himself as the Commercial Secretary, whilst the smaller man beside him was the Cultural Attaché. The women were their wives. One of them explained that some were renting flats in London, whereas she and her husband rented a small house because they had children. Sable was impressed and actually glad to be away from the attention of Gerit.

Something then caught her eye. "Who's that over there, in uniform?" she asked.

"He's our Military Attaché. He's a colonel in our army," replied one of the wives as she immediately recognised him.

Sable was impressed. She noticed that the colonel had a kind, handsome face. He was slim, tall and mature, with an air of confidence – an ideal husband for someone, she thought. She suddenly wished she was older and he was single.

The same Dutch wife was curious to learn more about Sable. "Do you have a job or profession?" she enquired.

Sable smiled. "Actually, I'm a student, reading languages – moving to Berlin in a few days' time. I met the Dutch PM in Paris. He invited me here."

The Dutch wife realised that Gerit, who had something of a reputation in Holland, and on the European circuit, was probably up to his old tricks: inviting young ladies to parties and functions.

"A word of caution, my dear," said the Dutch lady, "just be on your guard. He's a little bit like that American president who got into so much trouble."

Sable glanced across in the direction of Gerit Schmidt, then turned back to the Dutch wife who had been joined by a friend. "Madam, thank you for your kind advice, but I think I can cope with most people when I have to."

Both ladies smiled at her. This remark of confidence would come to stand her in good stead in the future. Sable could be tough when she needed to be. Her friend, Maria, had witnessed that.

The Dutch leader wanted to get away and have another chat with Sable. However, he was surrounded by a group of young Dutch politicians who were on a visit to London. Sable drank her champagne and then picked up a refill from a passing waiter. She was then greeted by a young Dutch girl who introduced herself as the ambassador's daughter. She slowly escorted Sable back towards the ambassador, explaining how successful the evening had been. The Cultural Attaché in particular had made some useful contacts.

"My dear, have you had a successful time here? Has it been useful?" asked the ambassador, with a matronly smile.

Careful to use the words 'Your Excellency' again, Sable explained that she had had useful conversations with several people, and of course, the Dutch PM.

Soon it was time to go home. Sable very politely said her farewells to all the official staff. She looked all round for the Dutch PM but he was nowhere to be seen. She therefore departed by both bus and then Underground. She picked up the evening paper to read on the way home. She also thought about the Dutch PM. He appeared to be a gentleman but his strong blue eyes were at times worrying. She also wondered if he was single; the remarks from those embassy wives were not totally clear.

Once back home, she answered all her mother's questions as well as she could. "So was there a real benefit in going?" asked her mother.

Sable responded by saying it had been a useful social experience, she had met some senior diplomats and had spoken to some interesting Dutch wives. The Dutch PM said he might see her in Berlin, she added.

"Ah, he's just talking, darling. Now the best thing you can do is finish packing for Berlin and send a message to Henri. You really must keep in touch with him. Give him your address in Berlin," ordered Gloria.

Henry Fairfax was working on some papers. He left all these domestic details to his very capable wife, but it was he who supplied the money.

Sable sorted out her German books. She knew she would be given extra papers at college. She still thought that two suitcases was quite enough. Her mother agreed.

9

At the end of the week she was all ready to go.

"Have they chosen a good college for you, darling?" asked Henry, just before he left for the office.

Sable assured her father that she was going to the best German language school in Berlin, complete with its own campus. It was situated in east central.

"Make good use of your time, darling, and phone us when you have settled in," he said as he departed for London.

Gloria drove her daughter to Heathrow for the flight to Berlin's Tegel airport. The weather was clear and cold.

After she had checked in, and boarded the plane, she noticed some young students, like herself. She wondered if they were going on holiday or to study German. A bit of a long shot, she thought, but she might find out.

After landing at Tegel, thankfully with her luggage, she boarded the Express bus into the centre and Alexanderplatz. As she looked out of the window she began to appreciate the modern buildings in central Berlin, symbol of a city risen from the ashes of both the Second World War and the long Cold War that followed almost immediately after it. She admired the Victory Column, built to celebrate military victories over the Danes, Austrians and, finally, the French during the nineteenth century. The latter was the victory in the Franco-Prussian war of 1871. Then she saw the Mercedes-Benz building. These were symbols of both the old and the new.

Once she had taken in the open space of the Alexanderplatz, with all its people, many of whom were waiting for a tram, she took the Metro. After a short ride she was close to Eberswalder Street in Prenzlauer Berg, the former East Berlin borough. It was here that she got off and took out her street map. She soon saw where she had to go. Pulling her suitcases, she carefully made her way on the gritted pavement to the college in Berlin's District 10435.

The college was pleasant enough, with its own campus, always a good sign. The building was modern and looked clean, unlike some of the drab Soviet buildings nearby. After checking in and registering, she was made to feel very welcome by the smart and cheerful German staff. She was escorted by one of the staff and given a quick tour of the essentials. This included her room and some of the facilities which were clean and tidy. It all seemed to be well equipped; she was pleased because she knew her father was paying quite a lot of money for all this. She was given directions of where to go for her evening meal and that there would be an assembly for all students soon

66

afterwards. Floor plans and timetables would be given out. They were also told that there would be an organised sightseeing tour of Berlin on the first Saturday. That pleased everyone.

At her first lecture, which was more of a school class, Sable realised that she was going to be given a lot of work. She was given fresh lists of verbs, plus tenses, grammar and vocabulary and all in the good cause of helping her on the road to speaking and writing mature, high-class German. She was still fascinated by the fact that all nouns commence with a capital letter. The various ways of writing the letter 's' had long intrigued her.

Her lecturers were mostly mature people, a mixture of male and female. One of her lecturers was elderly, with a chin beard and spectacles. She wondered how many changes he had seen during his lifetime, especially in Berlin. She would try to discover in due course.

When she phoned home to give her first progress report, her parents were pleased that their daughter was under pressure to work really hard and apply herself. It meant that Henry's money was being spent wisely.

When asked about the composition of her class, and the school generally, Sable emphasised the true nature of the mix of students. They came from Africa, the Middle East, South East Asia, Southern Europe and a few from England – the Midlands and Yorkshire.

"Is there no one from London?" asked Gloria.

Not on this particular course, Sable had replied. But she thought one had just departed.

The sightseeing tour of the city took in all the normal attractions: the governmental and public buildings, war memorials and churches including the Kaiser Wilhelm Memorial church, main avenues and shopping areas. They were shown where the infamous Wall had been plus the location of the old Reich Chancellery. They were also told that a part of the Wall had been preserved in the city. What was strange, however, was the view from the Reichstag to the new Chancellery building. It struck Sable as being rather a hideous, modern edifice, like a white blockhouse and only completed in 2001. They were informed by the guide that it was ten times the size of the White House.

Sable had by now made some friends. They were all in agreement that the building that had impressed them most was the Charlottenburg Palace, completed in 1713. The mixture of baroque and rococo was really impressive. The palace was located in the western part of the city. The guide also regretfully informed them that what was not on the tour was a visit to the city of Bonn; this had been the capital of the newly established Federal Republic of Germany in 1949. The old Palais Schaumberg building had served as the Chancellery building – and following reunification with East Germany, most government departments had relocated to Berlin by 1999. Bonn was really too far away. He also told them briefly about the work of the Allied Control Council which had administered Western Germany after the war and until the establishment of the new Federal Republic. Herr Konrad Adenauer was the first post-war new Chancellor in 1949.

Some of the students, who were generally lacking much knowledge of modern history of Europe, were busy taking notes. These were mostly the African students. They had only a passing knowledge of the development of western Europe, its politics or its military struggles. They were gradually learning that they were students in a city that was at the heart of a reunited country following the end of the Cold War. And the Soviet Union had been renamed Russia, following the fall of Communism.

They all bought postcards. Sable had three, which would be sent to Henri, Maria and her parents.

Sable asked the guide if there were guided tours to some of Berlin's bunkers. What she had read had intrigued her. On her map, in Mitte or central, he pointed to an area immediately north of the Spandauer Vorstadt. He said it was two stops north on the S-Bahn from the northern railway station or Nordbahnhof. Sable decided she would go there with some friends very soon and experience Tour One.

***

After each day she decided to learn some new pages of vocabulary. On the next day after rigorous lessons, she started. They were nearly all new words so she just sat down at her desk and started to memorise them. It was rather a challenge but after an hour she felt she had achieved something. Her next plan was to get her Chinese girlfriend in to test her. She was small, cute and was called May Ling. Sable knew that she was rather struggling with the course. Western languages were often not easy for South East Asian people to master. Similarly, Sable welcomed the fact that she was not having to learn Japanese, Mandarin or even Korean. It just looked so very difficult to understand the characters.

Sable and May Ling, in fact, progressed with the job that evening. Sable did well and surprised herself. She felt her confidence rising. But her dear Chinese friend admitted to Sable that she was finding the course difficult. It was just such a different language, often with long words. Sable extended her sympathy, told her that it was early days and she would help her to persevere. May Ling had found a true friend.

A few days later, after lectures, they all attended the student party. It was hosted by the college and the staff. After brief introductions, in both German and English, the students enjoyed German beer and soft drinks as well as some hot food. The sausages and hamburgers were the most popular. The students were encouraged to chit-chat in German and start seriously practising their new language. To put them all on the spot, the staff mixed and mingled and helped them where necessary – but English, or any other language, was forbidden. One or two of the more enterprising students were using dictionaries and phrase books to help them make progress. The staff were satisfied where they thought good efforts were being made. Sable knew that this would form part of her next progress report.

After another two weeks, Sable and three of her friends all went to visit some of Berlin's bunkers: the Gesundbrunnen Bunkers. Largely on Sable's recommendation, they chose Tour One: Dark Worlds. This tour explored a large, well-preserved Second World War bunker; it was one of hundreds of public bunkers that were used towards the end of the war by Berliners escaping from Allied bombing raids. It was on a very sombre note that their guide explained that in 1945 it was in this large complex of tunnels that many women, both young and old, committed suicide rather than be raped in their homes by the advancing Russian troops. For the benefit of the students who did not quite understand, their guide explained that some of the Russian troops had advanced across parts of Russia and had come across atrocities against civilians that had clearly been carried out by Nazi troops, often the SS. These Russian troops had fought their way into eastern Germany, before ending up in East Berlin as it surrendered to the victorious Russian Army. Raping the women was considered by some soldiers to be almost

71

their just reward for coming through it alive. These were the so-called 'spoils of war' and it was not new. Sadly, history was littered with it; most victorious armies in history were guilty of it. The guide pointed out that raping, and plundering, had taken place in Vienna, Prague and most of the cities and towns that had been savagely conquered. Sable remembered some of this from her history classes at school.

About a month later, when she was weekend shopping with May, she suddenly stopped at a newsagent. Something had caught her eye. She took her friend and showed her a photograph that was on the front page of both Der Spiegel and Die Welt. There was a mixture of both shock and surprise when Sable recognised the photo. It was the Dutch prime minister. He had been paying a visit to Berlin.

"His name is Gerit Schmidt and I met him in Paris," said Sable. "Oh goodness."

May Ling's mouth fell open with surprise. "You met a prime minister? Wow!"

Sable wondered where he was staying. She then went on to explain, as briefly as possible, how she had met Henri at the Sorbonne and had then visited the Hotel Matignon. She explained that Roland Tassier was the young French prime minister and the Dutch prime minister had been a guest.

May Ling could hardly believe that dear, ordinary Sable had met two prime ministers when most people might just dream about one. "In my country it is all so different, with a central party, a sort of one ruler, one state," commented May Ling. As they walked back to the language school, May outlined her ambition. She hoped she would speak German well enough to apply to her Foreign Department and become a junior diplomat. She would like to be posted to Germany or any other eastern European country where China had a consular or ambassadorial presence.

"I, too, would like to join our Foreign Office after university. And I can offer them French and, hopefully, German," Sable added with enthusiasm.

May Ling looked at her and tried to smile.

Once they were back at the school, Sable saw a member of staff. She suddenly remembered what had been on her mind. It was the Dutch embassy.

"Yes I know it," said the young lecturer. "On the north bank of the river Spree, and sort of south of the TV tower. An unusual design. You should go and see it." He then pointed at the city map on the wall. "It's here."

The girls studied the map and agreed to go on the following weekend. Sable wondered if the Dutch prime minister stayed there.

The next week in college was tough and demanding. They all had to give short presentations on a subject of their choice, but to keep it simple. They would then have to answer questions from their peers. They all knew it would require an awful lot of homework, with the traditional burning of a lot of midnight oil. May Ling was told that this idiom was a reference to the days when houses did not have electricity.

When they had written their texts, both Sable and May Ling had a dress rehearsal. They realised that it was going to be a pretty scary experience addressing a classroom full of their peers, eager to find fault. They were joined by some other students who spoke quite good English and who were keen to really improve their German. One boy explained that his father had to deliver lots of public speeches. His advice was, 'never rush it and always address the back row. That way you are seen to be treating your audience with respect; hopefully they will hear every syllable and learn something from your talk.'

It turned out to be not quite as bad as they had expected. Sable, May Ling and their friends all gained respectable grades for what the college described as a challenging assignment.

Back home, Gloria and Henry were so pleased that their daughter was making good headway. A routine note that they received in the post from Berlin, containing marks from their recent assessments, was satisfactory confirmation.

On the next weekend, Sable and May Ling were joined by an African girl called Jill Kamudona. Jill was one of the African students who was doing really well. She had lovely, long black hair which she used to tie up on her head and secure with silver clips bearing pearls.

She always looked attractive and never attended classes without her makeup. She wore deep red lipstick. Whenever she asked a question in class, she would stand up and make her point in what she hoped was a carefully-constructed German question. To the delight and intense surprise of the lecturers, she would remain standing until her question was answered. Sable thought that she was bound to end up top of the class. Everyone knew she worked long hours at her desk in her room and seldom went to any of the parties.

As they were walking towards the Dutch embassy, Jill explained to Sable and May Ling how lucky she was to be on the course. She came from Sierra Leone in West Africa which had become a really poor country, run by corrupt government officials. In fact, the United Nations ranked the country as one of the poorest countries in the world; it was also plagued by civil war which added to the poverty. She had been sponsored by several sources but it had been hard work to get all the money together. It was generally assumed that after her course she would work for the Foreign Ministry in Freetown in her home country. She would probably have dealings with both Germany and Austria and some of the Slavic states nearby, such as Slovakia. She would be making good use of her German.

May Ling thought that Jill had all the qualities of both politician and diplomat: she spoke well and in an authoritative voice. Perhaps she might enter the Civil Service in Sierra Leone.

Sable thought that Jill could do much better. She ought to come to England and consider the professions, such as law or accountancy; she could then join a large investment bank or a multi-national company that operated in Europe. She was too talented to stay hidden away in a West African country that was very reliant on aid.

"Oh my!" exclaimed Jill as they approached the embassy. The building that they saw had a slightly unfinished look about it. It was a cube that housed the ambassadorial accommodation, with office space.

They stopped someone who had come out of the building. He was happy to point out to these tourists that there was an enormous entrance hallway as a centrepiece where many of the staff worked. This extended up to all eight storeys and shaped the building's internal communication and ventilation system.

"Little privacy," commented May Ling.

Sable agreed, "It's all very open. You certainly couldn't have any secrets."

The Dutch gentleman listened to the comments with interest. Before he departed, this kindly gentleman indicated that it was a blend of security and formality of the Civil Service. "We live with it," he said.

"What do you think, Jill?" asked Sable, keen to have an African's views.

Jill thought for just a moment. "We are more used to old colonial buildings. I have to say, I don't really care for it. I prefer traditional rooms and corridors. But I suppose the staff just have to adapt to it in this modern world."

The Dutchman was about to depart when Sable remembered her question. "Excuse me, Sir, but is the Dutch prime minister staying here?"

He smiled. "Yes, he has been. He was on a visit to the German Chancellor and he combined it with a visit to a commercial organisation, as well as to one of the German manufacturers." He paused for a moment. "I think he departed yesterday."

Sable smiled gratefully at him. "Thank you, sir. Sorry to hold you up." And with that, the Dutchman departed, leaving the interested tourists staring at the cube.

10

Sable was unsure whether to tell her mother or not. She had not seen Gerit in Berlin so there was probably little point in mentioning it. In a way she was slightly disappointed, but then he did have more pressing matters on his plate, such as running the Netherlands.

They began their walk back to the college, taking in a few sights on the way.

Jill pointed. "May we go up there? It looks like a displaced satellite sitting on top of a huge factory chimney." They all laughed.

Jill was pointing at the TV tower, a huge transmitter, built during the isolationist years of the 1960s. The eastern part of the city had been inaccessible to West Germans; the tower was intended as a highly visible symbol of the permanence of East Berlin and the German Democratic Republic. They all agreed to go.

"Wow," declared May Ling, as she took in the fabulous view to the east towards the distant city of Frankfurt an der Oder and the border with Poland.

Sable was reading and told them that in 1945, when the Red Army reached the city, they found it empty. The city was then burned down. Since then it had been completely rebuilt.

"Tragic," commented Jill. "The civilians must have suffered enormously."

They all nodded agreement. Even May Ling was quick to realise the horrors of it all.

After leaving the TV tower, Sable and her friends walked to the north and stopped in Rathausstrasse. They wanted to make use of their time as tourists, so a visit to the Rotes Rathaus or Red Town Hall was a must. They all marvelled at it, largely because the Rathaus was badly knocked about in 1945, but made good progress following restoration work in the 1950s. Today the building houses the city's administration.

May Ling read from Sable's guidebook. She told everyone that reconstruction of the Rathaus, and thousands of other Berlin buildings, was largely due to the 'rubble women'. They had set to work in 1945 clearing up the one hundred million tons of rubble created by the wartime bombing and shelling. Women of all ages, she said, carried out the bulk of the early rebuilding work, since most of Berlin's adult male population were dead, disabled or were being held in POW camps by the Allies.

"Now that's what I call progress," commented Jill.

"I agree," added Sable. "It's amazing what can be done when it has to be done." Sable looked at the time. "Come on, let's get back."

***

They all worked hard and diligently on their course. Winter soon gave way to the early glimpses of spring.

May Ling worked the hardest because she still found German a difficult language. But Sable and Jill got on famously, tested each other and were surprised at the good progress they had made.

Henry and Gloria were keen to read the assessment marks from the college. In particular, Henry was impressed with the system: it put all the students on the spot.

Sable had received messages from Henri and was pleased that his course was going well. Her friend Maria told her what was happening in London – politics, entertainment, new shows – that sort of thing. Sable told Maria that they had occasional film showings in the college as a way of helping the students to comprehend how German was used in everyday life; lecturers would stop the film on certain frames and ask the students questions. It required severe concentration.

With the course coming to an end, Sable thought that a little more sightseeing for Jill, and especially for May Ling, would be sensible. With so much oppression still evident in the world, Sable had consulted the maps and location and decided that a visit to the former Reich Security office building would be sensible. May Ling had talked about lack of freedom in China and the consequences if you were seen or heard criticising the government. They could swiftly round people up.

First of all they went to see the former Air Ministry building. They found this on the south end of Wilhelmstrasse. It was more or less unscathed in May 1945. But it was now the Federal Finance Ministry. They admired the building before crossing over to the former Reich Security office.

"What was here, Sable?" asked an intrigued May Ling.

"The headquarters of the Gestapo and the SS," replied Sable.

May Ling was in the dark.

Jill came to the rescue. "Let me guess – the Secret State Police?"

"Exactly," said Sable.

They were looking at noticeboards which indicated sites of the most important Nazi, or NSDAP, buildings and revealed just how massive a machine the Nazi organisation became. They read that it was here that Himmler organised the Final Solution – the deportation and genocide of European Jews – and organised the Gestapo. The ground underneath the exhibition once held the cellars of the Gestapo Headquarters, where important prisoners were interrogated and tortured. Just around the corner was the SS Security Service Headquarters, where extensive records of all 'enemies of the state' were kept. This included Jews and homosexuals.

"I'm sure it happens in my country, too," admitted May Ling.

There was a pause for thought. It was Jill who commented. "But this regime was simply replaced after the war by another equally totalitarian state – the GDR. And did they have a secret state police?"

"Certainly did," answered Sable. "It was the dreaded Stasi. And they were just as bad, all operating under a Soviet-driven ideology."

They stood there, looking and wondering if mankind had made any progress at all.

"The better times must have begun when the Berlin Wall came down at the end of 1989," said Jill thoughtfully.

"And when East Germany was reunited with West Germany, soon afterwards," added Sable. At least she had remembered that.

May Ling nodded. She had at least heard that piece of news in China, probably from some of her friends. But world news was scarce.

They agreed to return to college. All three knew that they were firm friends and would keep in touch forever. Gloria would be happy for Sable to have such fine international friends.

When they were back at the college, the elderly lecturer was keen to know where they had been.

"Ah! Sightseeing. Soaking up history. Most important," he said. "And did you visit the Leipziger Strasse, the focal point of the building workers' uprising against the dreaded communist regime?"

Their faces said 'no'.

"It was June 1953. I recall it well. Sad days. Street fighting in East Berlin; bricks and bottles against armoured tanks, T-34s."

Sadness crept over the lecturer's face as he remembered those terrible events.

Jill was keen to know what the death toll was.

May Ling reminded them of China and the lone demonstrator who stood in front of a tank in Tianenman Square, full of defiance.

"Come into my study and I will check my papers and tell you all," said the kindly old gentleman.

The girls sat on the odd stool and rickety spare chair as the lecturer posted the death toll, as he saw it, on his whiteboard. "It makes depressing reading, even today. Oh, I should tell you, this demonstration was not just confined to East Berlin. About three hundred thousand workers, in two hundred and fifty towns, joined in. Anyway, in East Berlin traffic came to a standstill as a crowd of one hundred thousand people demonstrated against the GDR's communist Government. Two hundred and sixty-seven demonstrators, one hundred and sixteen policemen and eighteen Soviet soldiers were killed in the street fighting. Then, ninety-two civilians who had been arrested, were summarily shot. Additionally, eighteen Soviet soldiers were executed, most of them very young; they were aware of the terrible injustice that they had witnessed.

He stood there facing them. The facts were simply appalling.

Sable and her friends were totally shocked. "They never talked about this uprising in school history," said Sable, in defence.

The old lecturer nodded. "Believe me, this information, the figures, are relatively new data – all post 1989. But the other sad fact is that the western Allies did nothing to prevent this, nor the subsequent trials of 'counter-revolutionaries' at which fourteen death sentences were passed."

"No western intervention? Just condemnation?" asked Jill.

"Nothing physical. They just condemned it, obviously, but they did not intervene," added the lecturer. "I suppose they had to avoid a confrontation." It was a sombre moment to reflect on such a well-intentioned uprising and a very brutal response using tanks and bullets. He continued, "Some people have said that life under the communists was worse than living under the Nazis. Stalin was a brute."

Having taken it all in, they drew breath and thanked the lecturer for his time. May Ling had the last word. "So the western prime ministers were not prepared to intervene and stop what was, effectively, the murder of unarmed civilians. Is that correct?"

"You put it quite well," admitted the lecturer. "I suspect they were afraid of starting another war."

The three girls realised what a harsh regime the communist GDR had been.

" If Gerit Schmidt had been Dutch prime minister at the time, what would he have advised? I must remember to ask him," mumbled Sable as they filed out of the lecturer's room.

"We actually walked across the Leipziger Strasse," commented Jill as they walked down a corridor. She was looking at her map. "And what a shocking event – murder in the streets, and only a few years after the end of the war."

"I know," added Sable, shaking her head. "And all in the pursuit of fair and just pay."

They decided there was time for a quick meal before bed. As they sat at their table Jill was still shocked by it all. "Surely the American president and the British prime minister could have flown to East Berlin and put pressure on the GDR leader to stop any bloodshed?"

"You would have thought so, but would they then have been sucked into a conflict –a military conflict?" asked Sable.

May Ling spoke up suddenly, almost thinking aloud, "West Berlin, surely, was just an island of western democracy inside East Germany? They would not have wanted to risk losing West Berlin: it relied on the West, heavily."

Sable nodded, "Very true. Yes, well done."

Jill sat there shaking her head, almost angry that a government could do such terrible things to her own people.

As they left the refectory, they bumped into the elderly lecturer again. He smiled. He clearly had something on his mind. "I know you are all linguists, but I must just tell you that just three years later the same sort of revolt took place in Hungary. It was called the Hungarian Uprising of 1956. It started in Budapest. Again, there were terrible reprisals and bloodshed on the streets."

"That is just terrible," said Jill, showing concern again.

The lecturer continued, "And it occurred again in another country – this time it was the turn of Czechoslovakia in 1968. It was called the Prague Spring. Again, Soviet tanks were sent into the centre of Prague in August to bring order and restore stability in a tense and volatile situation."

May Ling was writing all this down in her notebook. So it wasn't just China that had dissenters, she thought.

He continued, "One young Soviet tank commander was told to quell a riot and was given a location. Apparently he had no idea that he had driven into the capital city from a rural area!"

Sable's mind had kicked in fully, as she recalled some of the modern history that Maria had told her.

"And what about justice for these poor people?" she asked, hoping it wasn't too stupid a question.

The lecturer's face was suddenly mournful. "Ah, my dear. You ask a very relevant and pertinent question.

You will discover that 'justice' is a commodity hard to find and sometimes so very difficult to achieve. In some criminal trials, never at all."

Sable was surprised. She went on the attack. "Well, I'll ask my father when I'm back in London. He's a solicitor."

"Excellent, but I think you will discover in life that the people who often escape justice are the politicians, often the world leaders. Some may be guilty of murder, even mass murder, but they are seldom brought to justice, as the saying goes. Goodnight." And on that sombre note, he departed.

The girls looked at each other, grateful that they had all learned so much in such a short space of time.

"I think it's time to sleep, and discuss this over breakfast." It was May Ling, speaking for them all.

11

"May I join you, please?" The three girls all welcomed him to their table. The elderly lecturer sat down to have his breakfast. "I regret I won't be seeing you much more. After your party, and prize-giving, you may be disappearing," he said in a kindly tone.

"We have greatly enjoyed meeting you," said Sable. "Your lessons have been so very interesting."

He smiled again and nodded his head in grateful appreciation of the accolade. "I thought I ought to just finish telling you a little bit more, especially about the reunification, after the Wall had come down." The girls were still eating but they listened attentively. "After an all-night Volkskammer session on twenty-third of August, it was announced that the GDR would become part of the Federal Republic on third October 1990. And on that day of reunification, Chancellor Helmut Kohl spoke to assembled dignitaries and massive crowds in front of the Reichstag."

"Were people happy?" enquired Jill.

"Generally, yes." He paused, before continuing, "then on twentieth June 1991, a Bundestag decision to relocate the national government, from Bonn to Berlin, ushered in a new era: a tremendous task, and one that was undertaken in the late 1990s with usual German thoroughness and efficiency. On the downside – a loss of manufacturing in Berlin, and a huge number of Berliners living on benefits. The legacy of state subsidies shoring up uncompetitive firms is said to be almost as detrimental to entrepreneurs in West Berlin as socialism was in East Germany. However, information technology parks in the southern suburbs have grown fast, as has the research and development sector."

They sat there, listening keenly. May Ling wished she was taking notes. She carried on eating.

But he had not quite finished. "Meanwhile, you will be pleased to know that tourism, part of our service sector, has become a major growth area, with Berlin overtaking Rome in terms of visitor numbers – making it third in Europe, after London and Paris."

"Now that is good news," remarked Sable, "and of course, a favourite location in which to learn the German language."

They all cheered and suddenly aroused the attention of the domestic staff behind the counter, some of whom were 'guest workers'.

As he finished his breakfast he got up to leave. "Enjoy your end of course party, and safe journey back home. Goodbye." He smiled heartily at them all and was then gone.

They sat there for a moment, finishing their coffee. In spite of almost loving her tea, May Ling had acquired a taste for coffee, once thought by some Chinese officials to represent western decadence.

They adjourned and went to their rooms to finish packing. A member of staff reminded them to be in the main auditorium at ten for prize-giving. All the students receive their certificates, together with details of their grades in the various modules. Eager to compare notes, they swapped information. May Ling's lowest marks were in translation from English to German. But she had worked really hard and her spoken German had certainly improved. She felt reasonably content.

Sable and Jill had both done well, but with Jill coming out top of her group. She was thrilled, and Sable so delighted for her. Sable knew that her improvement should enable her to do really well in her final year in London. Her mother should be pleased.

Later, they all spent an hour drinking beer and socialising with all the other students. They had all made lasting friendships and were somewhat sad to be departing and returning to their various home countries. They had all liked Berlin. The winter had not been too cold this year. The city looked grand in the early summer sun. The cranes here and there were a symbol of ongoing construction and development.

All three of them had assembled downstairs with their suitcases. Luckily their flights were more or less at the same time, within the afternoon hourly time frame. They said a final goodbye to the staff and walked out of the language school. They headed for the railway station that would take them to the airport bus stop.

As they stood there, they reflected on the fact that they were in the former East Berlin, with all its austerity, secret police, queues for food in the post-war years and little prospect of a bright future. Thank goodness mankind had swept all that away. All three girls were living in very different countries. Sable was about to return to a western democracy which had a habit of changing governments quite often. One of the drawbacks was often a lack of investment in certain projects, such as infrastructure – which was badly needed. At most, three terms in office was just about manageable for any government.

Jill was returning to her country in West Africa. It was poor, was heavily reliant on aid and was often plagued by civil war. Opportunities to develop the country were still somewhat limited. There was a diamond industry but development and investment here was thwarted by the risk of repeated guerrilla warfare. At least the foreign ministry would give Jill a warm welcome and a secure job.

May Ling was returning to China, with its stable form of communist government. She wondered whether she would be able to make a move to Hong Kong's Foreign Ministry. She knew it was worth a try. In spite of its faults, democracy and capitalism appealed to her, thanks to her time in Berlin. She also knew that there was a lot of truth in a statement that she had read, made by Mikhail Gorbachev: he said that the European Union was the old Soviet Union dressed in Western clothes. She knew that the EU was a dictatorship: the commissioners were appointed, not elected. There was also a huge amount of unproductive bureaucracy and corruption.

The girls all had each other's email addresses and phone numbers, so keeping in touch was not a problem.

Sable was the first to go. After hugs and kisses, Sable departed to her gate. She gave them a final wave before disappearing. As she went through security there were tears in her eyes, much to the concern of the attendant staff. She said she was all right as she forced a smile.

May Ling was in floods of tears as Jill did her best to console her. Jill decided she would improve her French once she got back home – she wished they could all work together in Paris. That would be a fine ambition.

The two girls were soon on their way.

12

Back in London, Sable had managed to find herself a summer job. She had two months to kill before resuming her course at London University. Actually, it was all down to her father, who had managed to persuade his firm to consider Sable in their Foreign department. They were usually receiving documents from their Paris clients, sometimes too many, and they all had to be read and identified quickly. Translation soon followed.

It was Gloria who had kept on pushing Henry to persuade the senior partners to open an office in Paris. Quite a few of their clients now had offices in both London and Paris. Sable knew she would be paid a lowly wage and it did not bother her. It was the experience that was so essential. Also, she was living at home.

Maria was really pleased for her. She suggested she could put it on her CV. The name of a City solicitor as employer would impress anybody. During the course of her time in the Foreign department she realised that she would be expanding her French vocabulary considerably. But there were just a few documents that were written in German. That was a bonus for Sable.

And so it was that some of the documents that crossed her desk were to do with such subjects as civil litigation, negligence in many forms, medical or professional negligence, and contracts. In the latter area, commercial contracts, often in the form of bulky documents, took up more and more of her time. Sable noted that the French jargon was impressive, and not too dissimilar from English. Her bulky French dictionary was in constant use, especially during her first few weeks of exposure.

One of Sable's tasks was to write a summary of each document in clear English and attach it to the front of the document. When she had done several, they were passed to the head of the department.

Sable did not join her father for lunch at all, preferring to sit with colleagues from her department. This was because they used to talk shop. It was a very useful way for her to learn something of the law, get used to deadlines and learn what not to talk about in the office. There was a culture to observe. The partners allowed small amounts of banter but generally they ran a tight ship in order to discourage idle gossiping and encourage maximum productivity. Essentially it required all employees to apply self-discipline.

Sable had missed most of the London social scene that summer because she had been in Berlin. Royal Ascot and most of the tennis had passed her by. At the end of July, she and Maria spent the weekend in Henley-on-Thames. They had gone there to walk on the chalk hills, to soak up some local history and to have fun boating on the River Thames.

They chose Saturday afternoon to go on the river in a tub. Sable drew the short straw and had to row - 'pulling her weight', as she called it.

"Darling, where's your friend Henri?" asked Maria, as she steered away from some inquisitive swans.

Sable thought. "He goes away in August with his parents. Down south, I gather."

"Most of France shuts down in August. All the factories close for a compulsory holiday," said Maria.

"I think he said that they were renting a cottage near the coast," recalled Sable as she pulled on the oars.

Still in the town, they were gradually moving upstream, thanks to Sable's efforts. When she wasn't answering Maria's questions, Sable wondered which of the two politicians was the most successful – the Dutch PM or the French prime minister. She knew that Gerit had more power than the French PM, but of the two personalities, she preferred Roland Tassier. He had some Gallic charm and wit. She had met Henri's mother, Brigitte, but she was still puzzled over Gerit. Sable was sure he had a wife somewhere: it was something that she had heard at the embassy party. And of the two men, she knew which one she would rather sleep with.

They pulled the boat into the side, moored it and then set about their picnic. As they ate their sausage rolls they admired the pleasure craft that went by. In one boat, with a family on board, they saw a mother wearing white gloves. She obviously knew the ropes when it came to the locks. Occasionally, the odd sculler went by. The girls marvelled at how they kept upright.

After telling Maria more about her student job in the City, and how she was enjoying expanding her vocabulary and phrases, and watching the solicitors take action, they decided to return to the town. They visited some old buildings, sampled the local brewery then went to their inexpensive hostel where they had an early night.

Next morning, they visited a chalk quarry and were amazed at the huge amount of flint it contained. Much of it had been used in the town.

"Good building material – it lasts forever," commented Maria with some authority as she pointed to a distant church. "Walls galore, but you never see it on roofs – must be too heavy."

Soon they were back in London and ready for the week ahead. Sable's workload eased off a little in August; there were fewer documents being sent over from Paris due to the holiday season.

When she left the firm in early September, she had definitely been of enormous help to them. She was sorry to depart: she liked the corporate environment. It was professional. They all wished her well at university and they hoped they would see her again.

Henry told Gloria that the senior partners had been impressed with their daughter's commitment, since she was only a student. "I keep telling her, it's all good experience," commented Gloria as she snuggled up in bed beside her husband. Her next move was to get on top of him and enjoy some much needed sex.

***

After her time away, Sable was soon back in familiar surroundings on the university campus. During her first tutorial she had discussions with her tutor on her progress in both Paris and Berlin. Her good progress was noticed. They hinted that if she worked really hard then she might come close to a First. They told her that she was very competent, with a good accent but her weakness was with certain aspects of oral German, such as idioms. Her translations, however, were very good. That pleased her.

During the first week, the college had organised a social event after lectures. This was to allow all the students who had been absent for the past year to mix and mingle and to exchange experiences. All those who had studied French and German were allocated one corner, whilst other linguists were in another corner of the large room. They were encouraged to use both languages where possible. Sable and others were able to chat in a relaxed way. She used her French more than her German. But when she encountered a student whose German was stronger, she tried hard to match it by practicing her German. The students had been all over

Europe. Lyon and Toulouse had also been popular for those studying French, while Frankfurt and Munich had proved popular destinations in Germany. Few went north to Hamburg.

Another task that they were all set had been to give a short speech on the benefits of studying in an overseas city. The students had been drawn by several factors: art, architecture, climate, history – even the cost of the course, for some less fortunate families. Sable and her peers had greatly enjoyed preparing and delivering their talks. In particular, when it came to highlighting Berlin as a language centre, she went to great lengths to bring in her knowledge of East Berlin and East Germany. She enjoyed talking about the politics. She was reminded of comments from her dear friends, May Ling and Jill, who had both contributed so much. She told the class how enduring friendships had developed for her. They were so important. She couldn't stress it deeply enough.

As she left college one day, she saw a news bulletin. It informed Londoners that they were hosting a forthcoming G7 summit later in the month. She went straight home to read her father's evening newspaper – he always brought one home. Gloria loved the gossip and the social columns. She had time to consult the political pages before their evening meal. She then realised it was best to go onto her computer afterwards in her room. She could combine it with her homework, of which there was never any shortage. She would also check her emails to watch out for messages from Maria and her other close friends. And she was always keen to hear from Jill, May Ling and Henri, who sometimes wrote in French.

She then wondered why she had never searched Gerit's biographical details. Simple. She had always been far too busy with other priorities. The data on Gerit Schmidt was quite interesting reading for a prime minister, but not unusual. It talked about his life at college then university. It gave details of how and when he entered politics and later became Leader of the Opposition. It described some recent visits overseas and the support that he would pledge for certain poor countries if and when he became Premier. It then said married, but gave no year. But the digital photograph did him justice – tall and handsome. Sable also discovered where in London the G7 would be hosted.

***

She caught a glimpse of the news as she stood in the bank. The world leaders were arriving in London. There were two banks that Sable often visited. One had a special clock on the wall near the counter, played music to its customers and also was equipped with a reasonable coffee machine. The other bank had a large TV screen behind the counter that showed permanent world news, but there was no free coffee machine. Not even a water dispenser.

Looking at the screen, Sable caught a glimpse of Gerit Schmidt as he was climbing out of a car. He was followed by his aides. He gave a broad smile, the one that she had witnessed at the embassy party. Later, there was coverage of the German Chancellor, wearing her customary dark slacks. To Sable, they looked like trousers and they made the German woman look very masculine. This was a woman who had been brought up in East Germany (DDR) under the yoke of the Stasi.

In college, Sable applied herself to her course and made sure she kept on top of her homework, especially the German. Writing essays required considerable application. She liked her lecturers, who ranged from young to mature. But there was no elderly lecturer quite like the one whom she had encountered in the language school in Berlin. That person had been full of history to impart to the young. If her peers wanted to discover London, they either had to walk the streets themselves or join one of the city sightseeing tours.

That night, back home, the telephone rang. It was just after eight. Gloria answered it. She was surprised to hear a foreign male voice asking to speak to Miss Sable Fairfax. When she asked who was calling, the voice stated that he was phoning on behalf of Mr Gerit Schmidt. "Just a minute, please. I think she may be in her room. I'll get her," replied Gloria. She put the phone down and ran up the stairs to Sable's room. She knocked gently and entered.

"Darling, there's a phone call for you. Someone on behalf of Gerit Schmidt."

Sable turned round. "Really? Good Lord. I knew he was in London – it's on the news." She ran downstairs and picked up the phone. "Sable Fairfax here. May I help you?" She listened as the polite Dutch aide introduced himself and explained why he was telephoning. He gave her the address of the hotel and looked forward to seeing her tomorrow night. Then she put the phone down.

Sable went into the lounge to tell her parents about the invitation. "Apparently he'd like me to join him for dinner after the summit is over. He's going home the next morning."

Henry and Gloria looked at each other. "Is it a big dinner party?" asked Henry.

"I've no idea, Daddy. It's probably a mixture of business and pleasure," replied Sable with a quick smile.

"It's something of an honour," said Gloria. "I mean, you have met him before. Does he have a wife?"

"Yes… Anyway, college finishes tomorrow in early afternoon."

"In that case you'd better go and enjoy it." Gloria smiled at her lucky daughter.

***

The Dutch aides escorted Sable into the private lounge in the hotel where the prime minister was staying during the summit. She wore a short black dress and, as usual, her hair was up. As soon as he saw her, Gerit broke away from his friends and came over to welcome her in. He gave her a kiss.

"Sable, I am so pleased that you could join us." He turned a little to indicate the party. "It's a mixture of politicians, civil servants and one or two business leaders." He escorted her over, gave her a glass of champagne and introduced her as the best linguist in the University of London. Sable smiled gracefully and was soon surrounded by two female Dutch civil servants who rescued her and put her at her ease. Sable noticed how Gerit kept turning to her and gave her a big smile as he spoke to his male guests.

Soon they were ushered in to dinner. There were two large round tables and it did not come as much of a surprise to find that she was seated on Gerit's left. Before they sat down she was impressed that there was grace, delivered by the PM himself. Then, as she sat there for a moment, she thought about Henri and wondered what he might be doing.

Gerit then turned to her and asked about her university course. When was she finishing? What were her plans? Sable pointed out that her French language skills would always have the edge on her German, but the university said that she was doing really well. She indicated again that there might well be a career for her in the Foreign Office. Failing that, there were always multinational companies looking for good staff, especially those companies that traded in France or Germany.

Gerit was impressed. "That's good, but have you considered a career in politics?"

She looked at him before taking a sip of her white wine. "I don't think that's for me, Gerit."

He nodded. "OK." He then looked at the menu. "The fish should be good – sea bass." He gave her another of his smiles.

Sable picked up the menu. There was also a red wine, and, of course, bottles of sparkling water.

As they were eating their fish he turned and clasped her hand as it lay in her lap. "Sable, you are so talented, please come and work for me in The Hague after you have graduated. There will be lots for you to do."

Sable was caught off guard and very surprised. But she knew it was an honour to be asked. She then reminded Gerit that she read German and French, not Dutch.

He smiled. "Don't worry. There will be plenty of work in your two main languages, plus the added advantage of learning a third language, Dutch. You'll find it easy. I'll ensure you are paid a good salary, and we might be able to give you a nice, yet inexpensive, accommodation. The bonus is that you'll see how government works: the interaction between politicians and the civil service."

"I'll certainly be happy to think about it while I finish my degree," she said with a smile. She made a mental note to consult Maria as well. She wondered whether this was a direct request to secure her professional talents or whether he wanted her for her personality and sexuality. And what about his wife?

"Does your wife get involved in politics, Gerit?" It was a very direct question and she hoped for a very honest answer.

He replied, very matter-of-factly, "Yes, she has to do much entertaining in the official residence and she sometimes has a look at my speeches, and improves them."

"But that's wonderful," smiled Sable in a very supportive manner.

He nodded before taking a sip of red wine. The meat looked very appetising.

Sable then spent some time chatting to a civil servant on her left shoulder while Gerit talked seriously to the aide on his right. One of the subjects that they discussed was the timing of breakfast in order to reach the airport on time.

The final course at dinner was cheese and celery. Gerit had asked for a selection of Dutch cheeses. He turned to Sable. "Did you know that all cheeses are named after the place where they are made? See here. Two small towns of Gouda and Edam in Holland produce these."

Sable nodded. "How amazing."

"By the way, Sable, you look stunning in that dress. It really suits you. The colour. And please, will you join me for a nightcap once we have dispersed?" Something inside Sable kicked in. She wanted to learn more about this man, and his intentions, so she said yes.

***

Back home, Henry and Gloria were watching the late-night news. Some of it had been taken up with the G7 and what they had agreed, and to some extent, preferred to disagree on.

"I wonder what time she'll be back?" asked Gloria, as Henry stroked her hair.

"Don't worry, darling, she'll come back in when it's politic to do so. She has a key," said Henry, reassuringly.

Secretly, they both wondered what the hell their daughter was up to.

***

When she needed to, Sable could wake up when she wanted to.

Without turning a light on, Sable could see it was five thirty. She looked across the large double bed and could hear Gerit sleeping. He was quite noisy. Like a cat, she slipped out of bed and dressed carefully, looking across at Gerit all the time. Once fully dressed, she carried her shoes and crept ever so quietly to the door. She stopped. She could see the big alarm clock. Taking a deep breath she inspected it and carefully turned off the alarm. She then tried the door. To her utter amazement it was not locked. He must have forgotten.

She crept out and found herself in the corridor once again. Putting on her shoes, she looked for the staircase. Locating it, she went down to the entrance hall. Not wishing to draw any attention to herself, she walked to the revolving front door which was activated by the smart man in hotel livery.

"Have a nice day, madam," he said, as he raised his hat.

"Thank you," she said.

Sable found herself on the street. She shivered in the cold of dawn. Then she walked until she found the nearest Underground station. Her plan was to catch an early train out of Waterloo. She just hoped everything was open. She looked at the time. With a bit of luck she might be able to join her father for breakfast.

A few days later a small column in his evening paper caught Henry's eye. It appeared that the Dutch PM had been late leaving his hotel in London. A spokesman jokingly said that his alarm clock had failed to go off.

***

Sable and her peers worked hard at their degree course and it was suddenly Christmas. She exchanged special messages with Jill and May Ling. In her spare time, May Ling said she was learning all about the history of Hong Kong.

Henri was spending Christmas in Paris. He told Sable what it was like inside the Elysee Palace. He had been on a special visit.

When she consulted Maria about her friendship with Gerit, Maria said it sounded genuine enough but she warned Sable to 'tread carefully'. There were politicians who possessed some sincerity and those who were completely lacking it. The latter were also sheer hypocrites. But Sable did receive a Christmas card from him, so she sent a friendly one back.

Henry and Gloria did not mind their daughter knowing the Dutch PM but they thought the Foreign Office was probably a better employment route for Sable. They encouraged her to start making enquiries in January. She might have to take Civil Service exams after her degree course.

Henry's job was going really well in the practice. They had some high profile clients which kept him very busy. Henry's business objective was to work either until he 'dropped' or until he felt like working part-time. He liked his job and he loved the City and he loved the family.

Sable went to a few parties over the Christmas period. She watched the New Year's Day concert from

Vienna and then spent the afternoon in her room doing a difficult and demanding translation. Later, her dear and close friend, Maria, came round to have supper with them all. The subject of the Dutch PM was touched upon. Maria also thought Sable would enjoy a career in the Foreign Office – a much more secure route.

By Easter, Sable was preparing for her examinations; she stayed in London. She had orals to worry about and she needed to revise her French idioms.

She had been keeping in touch with Henri and knew that he was similarly under exam pressure. That suited her because she wanted to exclude everything until the exams were over, and that also included Gerit.

Gloria insisted that Sable have a good breakfast every day during her exams. Gloria got up earlier each day to cook her daughter something sensible, such as sausages, sliced tomatoes and mushrooms. They were always preceded by muesli and milk.

***

Sable was one of several students who erupted with joy when the Finals Honours list was put on the noticeboard. She had gained an excellent Second Class Honours Degree in Modern Languages. The students were hugging and kissing; they were so excited that this hard work was now behind them. And what of the future? Some would go on to do a Masters, while others would go into a job.

Sable went straight to see her tutors to thank them for their kind support. They were most appreciative that she had done this. They even asked her if she wanted to stay on and take a PhD. Somewhat overcome, she said she would give it some thought.

Many of the other students went to the nearest pub to get drunk.

On her way home, Sable sent messages to Jill in West Africa and to May Ling. She actually thought that May Ling was taking a short holiday in Hong Kong.

At home, she broke the good news to her mother. She was rapturous and so delighted for her daughter. Gloria immediately made certain that there was a bottle of champagne in the fridge which Henry would open before dinner. And Maria would also be invited but, sadly, not Henri. He was just too far away.

BOOK TWO

13

It forms the main building in King Charles Street in London and it was built by a person called George Gilbert Scott. This was the Foreign and Commonwealth Office. It was completed in 1868 as part of the new block of government offices which included the India Office and later, about 1875, the Colonial and Home Office. The idea was to present a kind of national palace or drawing room for the nation, with the use of rich decoration to impress foreign visitors and dignitaries, especially in the India Office. It was hardly surprising that it would become a Grade I Listed building. This was the impressive and overwhelming edifice that Sable entered as she went to attend her interview.

Taking on board her mother's advice, Sable wore a black jacket and skirt with a white blouse. She wore clear stockings and black high heels. It may have been October but it was mild and dry.

The panel had been most impressed with Sable's progress at university and they were very interested also to hear her experiences in Paris and Berlin. They were pleased that she had a reasonable interest in politics and nothing further. Sable stressed that she wanted to utilise her French language skills and be of maximum use to the government. The gentleman on the panel just kept nodding each time Sable made a valid point. Whereas the elderly lady, who wore a dated tweed suit, never seemed to stop writing. The panel chairperson from human resources was keen and bright and asked most of the questions. Only once did Sable have to come out with a long sentence in French – which seemed to satisfy everybody. And the fact that her father was also working, went down well.

Sable had read a little about the building, which impressed the panel; she was then told that the rolling programme of restoration and refurbishment, carried out some years ago, not only brought many of the large rooms and other public areas back to life, it had produced much extra usable space and for far less than the cost of demolition and rebuilding.

After a long interview, which she hoped went well, she was shown the Durbar Court. Located at the heart of the India Office, it was the masterpiece of Matthew Wyatt.

"It was originally open to the sky," boasted the chairperson. "But no one liked the snow!" She then went on to point out to Sable that the four sides of the Court were surrounded by columns and piers supporting arches. Some of the columns were of polished red Peterhead granite, while the top floor Corinthian columns were of grey Aberdeen granite.

"What's this?" asked Sable as she pointed to the floor.

"Greek, Sicilian and Belgian marble."

They carried on with their walk until they had seen most of the highlights. Sable was then taken back to reception and reminded that the Court was first used in 1867 for a party and reception for the Sultan of Turkey.

Sable arrived back home and immediately told her mother all about it. From the way she spoke it was obvious to Gloria that Sable had been tremendously impressed with the place.

"So what will happen?" asked her mother anxiously.

"If they like me, they'll take up references, mostly university. Then I'll just have to wait on the postman," said Sable. "Meanwhile, I'll try and find a temporary job."

Gloria had a brainwave. "Let's ask Henry. I wonder if their Foreign Department could use you again?"

Sable smiled. "Brilliant... I'm going up to change. I think they approved." She pointed to her suit as she went upstairs. 'Why not phone the Foreign Department myself,' she mumbled as she entered her bedroom.

Six days later Sable found herself being welcomed back into the Foreign Department. One of the staff had been sent to the Paris office for a short assignment, leaving a larger mountain of unfinished work than expected. Sable's first task was to translate the first two sections of a bulky report – it was in French. She was told that the contents were rather technical in places, so accuracy was essential. The report was likely to form part of a Court bundle of documents in a forthcoming civil trial.

Sable was shown to the empty desk. Her task was to translate onto a computer and produce a document. Keeping her French dictionary and her law dictionary close to hand, Sable was pleased to be helping the firm again.

Somehow her supervisor had discovered that Sable had been to the Foreign Office and was waiting on news. But she also recognised that Sable was very professional as well as being an accurate translator. If they lost her, the government would be gaining a good member of staff.

Sable was fascinated with the nature of the documents: some were to do with Contract Law while others fell into the Torts category. There was a report from a hospital where an operation had gone wrong, some engineers who appeared to have been responsible for a weak bridge, and some financiers who had given sloppy advice to investors.

Her work went well and the days passed by. At the end of the third week, on the Friday, Sable was persuaded to attend a drinks party in the office for someone leaving. After the presentation, they all repaired to a City watering-hole where rooms had been reserved for them. Sable said she would stay for just one hour. During that time she met some of the female solicitors, with whom she got on well. She told them that many of the technical words were just the same in

English as well as French. She also thought there would be similarities with German.

Before she departed, one of the solicitors from another department introduced himself. They shook hands.

"What do you do?" she asked. She wanted to know his role or function.

"I make money," he said and then laughed.

He was quite good looking but Sable was more interested in going home. "I'm sure you do. Solicitors and barristers are not cheap."

"Yes, that's true," he said. "Would you like some champagne? I know a good place not far from here." He looked at her. He liked what he saw.

She smiled. "That's most kind – perhaps another time. I really do have to go. Goodbye." And with that, Sable walked purposefully to Bank station, happy to be going home. The party had been good but she really didn't know many people there. She was only temporary, not a full member of staff.

Once home, Gloria took her immediately to her place at the kitchen table where she kept incoming mail. She handed her a large brown envelope marked 'Foreign and

Commonwealth Office'. "Darling, this weighty package is for you."

They both sat down and Sable opened it carefully. She withdrew the contents, on top of which was a covering letter. As Sable read the first paragraph it was clearly good news. She reached the end, then jumped off her chair with sheer delight and punched the air with a loud 'yes'.

Her mother hastily read the letter. It was the offer of a position in the Foreign Office where she would commence making use of her specialist skills. There would be five weeks of mandatory training and she would be encouraged to make a career in the Diplomatic Service. Her initial focus would be on European matters.

"I sensed it was a positive interview – but you never quite know, do you?" said Sable with a happy smile.

Her mother gave her a hug of congratulations. "Wait till Daddy sees this. Your references must have been good."

Later on, they all looked at both the letter and the enclosures. It gave her a start date and the booklets described all the benefits of working for the government in the Foreign Office. It also mentioned how new staff were encouraged to think about the Civil Service as a long-term career and to study for the exams.

"Gosh, more exams," said Sable, with a slight sigh.

Henry was positive. "Don't worry, darling, you'll probably find it quite easy and very relevant. I expect you'll be in our embassy in Paris in a few years' time."

That could be good, she thought. "I might see Henri."

"And think of all the other French-speaking countries of the world," her mother added enthusiastically.

"And one day you might become an ambassador," reflected Henry. He then became serious. "Let it sink in over the weekend and start to compose your acceptance letter on Sunday. Don't delay, darling. They obviously need you."

Sable was happy to take her father's advice. He decided they would all go out to lunch on Sunday to celebrate. That evening she telephoned Maria to give her the good news.

When she was back at the firm on Monday she went in with renewed vigour and confidence. The government wanted her and they had offered her a very reasonable starting salary. She could also take advantage of a season ticket loan in due course.

She spent the morning at the spot where she had left off on the previous Friday. And at lunchtime she posted her acceptance letter to the Foreign Office using first-class postage. She knew she was on her way. She had also made a note in her diary of when to visit her contact in personnel and give them the good news.

Also in her lunch hour, she sent short emails to both May Ling and Jill giving them brief details of her good news. She said she would write more fully later. She waited until she got home before sending an email to Henri.

It was when she was at home that she suddenly remembered the job offer from the Dutch PM. She knew that politics was often a dodgy and uncertain trade so she decided to forget all about him, at least for the time being. He was probably just trying to be helpful.

Her week at the firm was productive and satisfactory. Apart from just doing her job, she had also helped a few other people out, including a French lady who was unsure whether to proceed with some litigation or not. On Friday she warned personnel that she was likely to be leaving soon; and on the following day her letter from the Foreign Office gave her detailed joining instructions. She would go to a room in King Charles Street.

The City firm would not let her go without informing her that she would always be very welcome back there, even in retirement. The door would always be open to her. They also gave her a small present: it was a small black handbag designed for evening parties. After she had opened it, and had made a very small but cheerful speech, the head of litigation said it was just large enough to hold a small pistol. Everyone laughed. Even Henry, who had been pulled out of the Business Department, thought that was very funny.

***

And so it was that she entered King Charles Street.

Sable had been working well and had been getting used to the formality of the Foreign Office. She immediately sensed there was a rather specific culture and it was her duty to become acquainted with both culture and convention as quickly as possible. After further discussions with personnel, she said she would be happy to embark on Civil Service training in due course – and most happy to train towards becoming a diplomat.

Her first few weeks went well, much to the delight of her parents. There were all sorts of queries to deal with, letters as well as emails that required attention. Luckily the staff canteen had a good range of dishes.

Maria was fascinated with the detail. She lived in west London and had a much less grandiose job, in accounts. She just hoped that when Sable was on a suitable posting overseas, she could go and visit her or even stay with her.

Sable naturally agreed to attend the Christmas party for Foreign Office staff. It was usually held at a reasonable London hotel. By now she had got to know some of the other female staff and she was invited to join a table and make up a foursome. They were all single girls.

On the night of the party, the table turned out to be much larger and they shared it with four other people. They appeared to be couples. But that did not bother them at all. The tables were covered with huge white tablecloths plus bottles of red and white wine.

One of her friends, Marion Large, recognised one of the men. "That's Harold Jones. I don't really know the others."

Sable liked to practice her German with Marion. Her other friend, Madeleine Topper,was well versed in Polish and Russian. She told them all that she had visited Warsaw and Moscow as a student. Summers over there were hot, she said with a grimace. The fourth girl in their team was Kate Smith. She was petite, with short black hair. She spoke Mandarin and quite good Japanese. She loved the sushi bars in London.

Once the dancing was under way, Sable suddenly discovered a pair of legs beside her chair. She looked up and saw it was the man called Harold Jones. He smiled. "May I have this dance with you, please?"

Slightly uncertain, Sable got up and joined him on the dance floor. She glanced at Marion, who gave her a reassuring smile.

"I'm Harold, but please call me Harry," he said.

"Sable," she said, and that was it. The music was just slow enough for them to hold each other.

"They always do give a good Christmas party," he said.

"This is my first." She looked at him, slightly quizzically. "Who are your friends?" The music was Glen Miller. Sable liked it.

"Oh. Well, friends. We're all Civil Servants. How about you?"

"I'm going to train to become a diplomat. French and German are my languages. My friends over there are also linguists. Marion speaks German too. And I just loved Paris and Berlin when I was there." He nodded. She looked up at him. He had well-groomed, dark brown hair and he was close-shaven. That pleased her. She hated beards.

"Do you like art galleries? We could go to the Tate, the old one, at a weekend," he said as he narrowly escaped treading on her toes.

"Yes, there's always something new to see," she commented. They continued to chat and dance. She noticed that her friends were watching her keenly but had not got onto the dance floor yet – no partners.

When there was a break in the music, she took Harry back to her table and quickly introduced him to her friends. She used the word Harold as it sounded better.

Suddenly her phone rang. It was immersed in her handbag. It was Maria. She quickly excused herself and left Harold to talk to the girls. He sat down amongst them and started chatting.

"How's the party going? Have you met anybody nice?" Maria asked.

Sable chuckled. "I've had my first dance – with someone called Harold, although some people call him

Harry. No one else on the horizon yet. The night is still young."

"And the meal?"

"Beef Wellington," recalled Sable.

"Lucky you. Will you have another dance with him?"

Sable pondered, "I might – but there are three other girls at my table, all single." Not wanting to hold her up any longer, Maria wished her dear friend a lovely time.

Sable walked back to the table to find Harold sitting amongst the maidens. As soon as the music started up again, Harold took Madeleine by the hand and led her onto the dance floor. It was a fast number; Harold loved it but Madeleine hated it. Sable watched as poor Madeleine struggled. As soon as Sable caught her eye, she beckoned to Madeleine to come and sit down.

Making a polite excuse, Madeleine did just that. "Thanks, Sable. You've saved me." This was not Madeleine's thing at all. She liked waltzes.

Meanwhile, Harold looked to see if someone on his side of the table was keen to dance with him. But they were all in deep conversation. "Shit," he said lightly. He sat down and waited patiently. Then he looked across at the other girl, the one who spoke Mandarin. She was the small one, with black hair. After she had stopped chatting he might just ask her for a dance.

An opportunity came. Sable and her friends were soon watching as Harold and Kate Smith swayed gently to the music. He seemed to be almost hugging her. As

Sable regarded them, she realised that Harold had a kindly face. She wanted to know what his qualifications were. Kate was short. Her face was almost on his chest and Sable wondered how much lipstick was on Harold's shirt! However, Kate's dress was a lovely colour, a deep blue and it went well with her black hair and deep red lipstick, or what was left of it.

Suddenly one of the girls from the next table deposited three bottles of wine on their table. Sable and her friends looked surprised.

"Surplus to requirements. Please enjoy them."

They all looked at the bottles, this unexpected present. Marion read the labels. "Not bad. Let's get on with it." She poured red wine into the two glasses and offered the white wine to Sable. It really was Christmas.

At the end of the dance, Harold brought Kate back to her seat. It had gone quite well but she was obviously glad to sit down again. Seeing her glass had been replenished, she took a long sip. Sable smiled at her.

"He's quite an ambitious dancer, but I think one's enough," laughed Kate. She was soon halfway through her red wine. "Mm," she gasped.

The party had been good. If this was a sample of what her employer offered staff each year, then Sable was happy enough. She wondered what it was like at the Grosvenor House Hotel. Her father had spoken highly of it.

At the end of the evening they all gathered up their belongings and went to fetch their coats. Once outside, the girls started chatting and saying their farewells. They would all be seeing each other on Monday morning.

Harold caught up with Sable, as the girls were walking to either bus stops or the Underground.

"That was a fun evening. May I escort you to Waterloo? It's my station. How about you?"

He looked for a lit-up taxi.

"Yes, it's actually my mainline, too. Thanks, Harry."

Harold had soon flagged one down and they were quickly making their way along the Embankment. He sat beside her and admired her. She caught his eyes. "The city looks good when it's lit up like this. Don't you agree?" he asked.

She nodded. "It's full of sparkle."

He then became slightly more serious. "So whereabouts are you located, where is your office? Or is it a big secret?"

She laughed, then described her location as best she could. She realised then that her office was a long way from Harold's. But it did not matter; probably an advantage.

He told her a little bit about his work and she was suitably impressed. Apparently, he had to attend quite a lot of meetings. "I've developed my own brand of shorthand. Had to," he said with a chuckle.

Once they had arrived at Waterloo Station they soon found themselves on the main concourse. It was quite busy. "Theatregoers," he said. "May I have your phone number, Sable? We've got to do the Tate one day."

She made a point by firmly telling him that it had to be for 'after work hours only'.

He promised he would respect that. He went up to her and thanked her for the lovely dances and for helping to make it a fun and memorable evening. He wanted to kiss her but thought he would delay that.

She sensed what he was thinking. "My first party, as you know. The first of many more, until I'm sent overseas," she said. "Look, there's my train. Talk next week." And with a flourish she ran for her train, convinced it was about to depart. Harold looked up at the notice-board: she had ten minutes in hand. He smiled.

14

Over the weekend, Sable recounted the events of the Christmas party to her parents, who were keen to know more about it. Gloria, in particular, wanted to know more about the girls at her table. She also wanted to know more about Harold. Sable thought he was genuine enough. She was convinced that he lived in West London somewhere and he was obviously senior to her in the Foreign Office. Gloria wanted to know which university he had attended. Sable said that he seemed keen to take her out to the Tate gallery, at which point she would try to discover more about his background.

"Darling, just ask him a few questions – do it over tea, after you've viewed a few paintings."

Always sensible advice, Sable acknowledged.

The following week at the office found Sable doing a lot of extra work: her immediate superior was away. She had temporarily forgotten that he was on a short course, organised by personnel, on 'management development'. Part of it was to do with decision-making. It was held at their facility to the west of London.

Sable found herself using more and more German. Some papers had come in from the Department of

Trade, which in turn had come in from one of their offices in Germany. Much of the paperwork had to be translated, according to a memo. She realised that she might have to cut her lunch hours short and work until six if necessary. She phoned her mother to warn her.

"Don't worry, darling, it's bound to filter down onto your staff report." Henry knew that large organisations had staff reports – it kept personnel busy and helped to chart the progress of rising stars.

The language was pretty formal, so Sable was able to type from German into English quite easily onto her screen. She used her dictionary less than she was expecting to. She thought her tutors in Berlin would have been suitably impressed. This reminded her: she owed them an email of her career progress.

Two weeks after the party, and a few phone calls later, she found herself admiring some of the delights of the Tate gallery. Harold had met her there. They had been into many of the rooms, viewing portraits, battle scenes and landscapes. But she particularly admired the works of the Pre-Raphaelites, Holman Hunt and Sir John Millais in particular.

And then she saw something that took her straight back to her school days. It reminded her of how her teacher of English poetry had waxed lyrical over the poem, 'The Lady of Shalott', by Alfred Tennyson; of how easy it was to understand, so long as you were prepared to expand your English vocabulary and learn about gardens and waterways, and remember myth or legend of many-towered Camelot and the knight, Sir Lancelot.

"Remind me, Sable, who painted this? It's a huge canvas," Harry enquired. He was quite happy for her to call him Harry – everybody did.

Sable was captivated by the painting by John Waterhouse in 1888. He had been a member of the Pre-Raphaelite movement, she told him. "Harry, this is a beautiful interpretation of The Lady of Shalott from the famous English poem by Tennyson. Ultimately, it's a sad story. But examine the colours and the detail: what she is wearing and the boat in particular. Look at the lantern. It's all rather lovely and fine, yet this poor girl is doomed to die. A curse is upon her."

Harry turned to her, impressed. "I thought you were a linguist?"

She smiled. "English GCSE. I've never forgotten it. I mean, how could you?"

"Yes, quite." Harry continued looking at the painting, trying to be appreciative. "Poetry was never my thing but I'm sure we touched upon it."

Sable looked around. "And I just love the Pre-Raphaelites. They are so distinctive. There's one in the Guildhall Art Gallery. And I think Daddy was at school with a descendant of Millais."

Again, Harry turned to her, impressed. "Really?"

After examining another room full of impressive paintings, Harry decided it was time for a pot of tea – England's finest.

They were soon seated and she was pouring into two white cups.

"Well done," he said.

She looked at him as she sorted out the sugar. "Tell me, Harry, what did you read at university, and where?"

He did not hesitate. "London School of Economics and Political Science, to give it its full name. Haughton Street. Do you know it?"

"I've been into the student union," she admitted proudly. "And ...?"

"Economics and Politics, with subsidiary French. I also know a little Arabic."

"Now that will be useful," she said with emphasis.

"It's how I got the job, I think," agreed Harry. "And I'm willing to have more lessons before they send me overseas – Middle east, North Africa, who knows?"

"One is almost waiting for a crisis to happen; once there's diplomatic activity, messages start coming in," said Sable. "My father remembers the days of cables and telexes."

"Faxes are still used, quite widely, apparently. Damn clever," added Harry. "You get an instant print."

He picked up the plate of cakes and offered them to Sable. She took two light sponges.

"Where did you learn your Arabic?" she asked.

"We were overseas for a while. I was quite young, learnt it in the classroom, mostly. We had servants."

"Lucky you." Sable enjoyed her first cake with her first cup of tea.

"And where were you schooled?"

"Boarding school, eventually. It was quite fun. Then after A-levels, I set my sights on university. I wanted to remain in London so the LSE was an obvious choice. They do actually have quite a range of subjects there – languages, humanities, law etc." He picked up two pieces of chocolate cake. They looked good.

"Do you remember your interview, Harry? Did you have a panel?"

He sipped some tea. It was hot. "Yes. Don't they always? I'm sure it's standard procedure."

She continued to ask him questions in an effort to know him better and to paint a decent picture for her mother. He appeared to be an only child, like her. He was clearly set on a career in the Foreign Office. She hoped he would go far. She approved of ambition.

Once tea was over, they gradually made their way out. Harry thought they had soaked up enough culture to last them several months; as far as Sable was concerned, she could do the whole thing again next weekend.

Soon they were in Pimlico. Harry was looking for a bar. "Let's have a drink before we have dinner."

She smiled. "Fine."

They found a decent little place tucked away down a sidestreet that was not too busy. They discovered that the customers were a mixture of tourists and Eastern European immigrants. While Sable secured two places on a corner couch, Harry bought a glass of white wine and some stout for himself. They were soon chatting away, discussing current foreign policy, amongst other topics. As far as Harry was concerned, it beat Tennyson.

She told him all about her life at school, her parents, university and her time in the European capitals. She conveniently omitted Henri, the Dutch PM and some of her other adventures and escapades.

While she was talking, Harry glanced across circumspectly at some of the other girls in the bar. There were some rather nice Asian girls who were all in a group having a bundle of fun. He liked their short skirts. He suddenly wanted to be with them and buy them all drinks.

Sable asked him a few questions about lines of command in the Foreign Office. This suddenly refocused his mind. He, in turn, asked her questions on international relations. She felt this was the province of senior advisors to the Secretary of State and senior diplomats. In addition to her languages, she would ensure this was included in her training, if her voice could be heard.

Before they left, he had a chat with the barman. Then, once outside, he steered her in a northerly direction. "Italian or Chinese? What takes your fancy?"

She thought for just a few seconds. "Ooh, well. Since I love cheese, it has to be Italian."

In no time at all they were ordering soup, made from large Italian tomatoes. And to follow, he ordered a huge pizza covered in cheese and sliced olives. "Just what the troops need after a long day," he said.

Apart from enjoying Sable's company, Harry's roving eye descended upon the only Asian girl in the restaurant. She was sitting with her partner, probably her husband at a guess. He wondered if the FCO would ever send him to somewhere such as Thailand or Vietnam so that he could feast his eyes on such girls. But he would have to learn the language.

"Jolly fine soup, Harry."

Her comment almost startled him. Yes, he agreed, it was rather good. He studied her face carefully as he chatted to her. In particular, he liked her eyes and her almost black hair. He then realised that she was probably not wholly Anglo-Saxon.

They attacked the pizza with enthusiasm. As they did so he wondered if there was any scope to have lunch with her in the staff canteen, say once a week. They would need to choose their best days. He hoped Wednesdays might be manageable: it was a good day for him. She said she would let him know.

"Do you know, a friend of mine is shortly being posted to Tokyo. I asked him if he would have difficulty with the language," said Harry.

"Is he with us?" she asked.

"No. No. Another company. He's in IT. Anyway, it's such an international city that everyone speaks English, would you believe. You only need Japanese if you plan going out into the countryside areas. That really shows you how dominant English is in the international business world."

She chuckled. "So the Japanese have to learn English instead?"

"I think it's compulsory in schools," said Harry. "They do a lot of trade with America and import most of their oil and gas from Arabia – so they have to converse or negotiate in English."

By that time the tasty pizza had disappeared. They only had room for coffee, so they both had white. She declined a brandy.

"We could see a play later in the month?" he suggested.

She nodded. "I've seen most of the musicals. But there might be one that's escaped me."

"I'll look around, shall I?" he suggested. She smiled in agreement.

It was late, but not too late, when they left the restaurant. It had been a fun afternoon for Sable; Harry had enjoyed the evening once they had finished admiring all the paintings in the gallery. He knew they were going in different directions. She guessed he was going to say something.

"Don't worry. You don't have to walk me home. Thanks for a lovely evening, Harry."

He gave her a gentle kiss on the cheek. "We'll see if we can have lunch sometime. Get home safely."

And with that, they parted. He strolled to the nearest Underground station while she made off towards Vauxhall Bridge. She would have to catch a stopping train from Vauxhall.

On the following day, her mother allowed her daughter a bit of a lie-in. When Sable eventually emerged into the kitchen, her mother made her a coffee and suggested that she eat a banana. Her father was in his study.

As Sable sat down, she prepared herself for a whole range of questions about Harold.

It soon became clear to Gloria that Harry was probably acceptable and was on a career path in the Foreign Office. That pleased Gloria. "He must have ambition. Just like you, darling," she commented.

Up on the wall in the kitchen, the TV was on. It was showing world news. Sable was suddenly aware that the CNN commentary was focused on the French prime minister. She heard the name Monsieur Tassier and suddenly there he was.

"Look!" Sable almost shouted. Gloria turned to examine the screen. There were scenes of Paris and the French PM. "That's Henri's father!" exclaimed Sable. "Where's Henri, mon ami?"

They were both transfixed by the news bulletin. The PM had been performing a task on behalf of the president, who was unable to attend. It said little more. Gloria turned to her daughter, still transfixed by what she had seen.

"Are you still in touch with Henri?" she asked.

"Why yes. Mostly emails. He's fine. Gosh. I must write and tell him how his father suddenly surprised us all."

Gloria poured another cup of coffee for her daughter, whose mind was now temporarily focused on Henri and not on Harold. Sable got up from the kitchen table and sat in the armchair at the end of the room. She picked up Friday's newspaper and busied herself.

She was about one third of the way in when a bold headline caught her eye. It was all about a divorce in the High Court in the Strand. An ex-wife was claiming a simply huge, almost grotesque sum of money from her former husband. Admittedly he had money to burn but that hardly seemed a reason for her to claim obscenely huge and vulgar sums of money to cover such items as handbags, scarves and shoes. The amount of money that she was claiming was, even in Sable's eyes, simply totally unnecessary extravagance.

"How long does a handbag last you, Mummy?" she called out.

"A handbag, did you say, darling?" Gloria thought for a moment.

"Weeks or months?" asked Sable.

"Years," replied Gloria.

Sable nodded. That's what she thought. So how come this spoilt brat was getting through handbags at a rate of knots? Sable read on and discovered that the list of 'needs' of this ex-wife was huge and, in her opinion, totally unrealistic. What kind of world was this woman living in? The judge was being asked to make an award so that she would continue to live the lifestyle to which she had become accustomed as the wife of a very wealthy husband and businessman. He was now living in Saudi Arabia, while she enjoyed the London house in fashionable Mayfair, complete with cooks, maid, gardener, cleaner and chauffeur-driven car. Sable wondered if this woman had ever used a train, bus or London Underground in her life! She also thought the judge was being weak. She then realised that he had to apply the law and determine how the spoils should be divided up. Sable also thought it was a shame the woman couldn't be ordered to go out to work and behave like a normal person. Perhaps that was being unkind. After finishing the article, she was ready for another drink – sparkling water would do.

"Anything interesting in the paper?" her mother enquired.

"Just a very expensive divorce case in the High Court," added Sable. She then pointed at the paper. "Some people need to live in the real world, I tell you. That woman is asking for simply millions. I think it's vulgar and obscene." She sat down to have a drink.

"Well spoken, darling. You know, if you hadn't gone into the Foreign Office, you could have trained as a solicitor and spent all your life handling high-profile divorce cases and made good money. People do, you know." Gloria had made her point by outlining an alternative career.

"Yes, but would I feel good about it?" Sable said aloud as she looked at the paper. Sable then looked at her. "I just think there's something unsavoury about making a fat living out of other people's misery, misfortunes – call it what you like." She nodded her head. "Anyway, my strengths are in my languages. I can help that way." Sable sat at the table, contemplating. "Acting for a client in their divorce: would I feel good about it?" The question was clearly rhetorical.

Her mother continued, "Darling, her expectation is that the marriage should have lasted, and had it lasted, her lifestyle would have remained at that high and expensive level. Am I right?" asked Gloria. Sable nodded a 'yes'.

"So why should she lower her expectations?" Gloria asked.

"True," admitted Sable.

"And tell me, when are you next seeing Harry?"

Sable explained that they were going to try to have lunch together in the canteen, possibly on a Wednesday, so long as it did not conflict with any business. They were in different departments but she thought something should be manageable.

Late on Sunday morning Sable went over to see Maria and have a light lunch with her. They talked about business and boyfriends.

Maria's job was fairly ordinary. She wished she had studied harder and become a chartered accountant.

Instead, she was an accounts assistant. She knew her job well but she knew she would never rise very high.

"Don't worry, darling, I'm sure they value you," said Sable, full of encouragement for her dear friend. Sable knew that Maria was dependable and reliable. She was also methodical. Maria knew that Sable was very supportive; in fact, it worked both ways. They knew that in times of crisis they would always look out for each other.

"So tell me about Harry. This sounds exciting," beamed Maria.

"It's early days but we are going to try to have lunch together soon, midweek – then he talked about a theatre trip some time. Yes. He's nice. Polite. But he's not too keen on art. I think I gave him too big a dose at that gallery." Sable laughed.

"Art's not really a boy's thing, is it?" suggested Maria. "But anyway, let's hope it goes well." She then paused for a while. "And tell me, what has become of Henri, your dear friend in Paris?"

Sable recounted the news bulletin on CNN and how she realised that the odd phone call to him would be sensible, in addition to her emails. She liked him, even if he was a trifle young.

"The son of a senior politician would be quite a catch, darling," commented Maria.

Sable nearly said 'for me or for him?' Instead, she nodded and smiled. "Well, they are rather nice parents."

"Keep him going, darling, you never know what can develop out of friendships – whichever side of the Channel." Maria smiled at her. "By the way, what's your Dutch friend, Gerit, up to these days?"

Sable thought for only a moment. "I've no idea. Running his country? Anyway, he's hardly my friend. More of an acquaintance, who probably wants to be my friend."

"Mm. Is he married?" Maria was wondering.

"Yes… It was kind of him to try to offer me a job, but, as I told him, I'm not into politics."

"Are the Dutch very religious?" As she said this, Maria got some drinks together.

Sable scratched her head. "I've no idea. Probably similar to us. Perhaps more Protestant."

Maria recalled her early days at school. "I was brought up into the Church of England. But it was really more of a formality. I mean, you fell into one camp or the other. At school, you know, they never really explained things very clearly – I mean, differences in faith. You were either Church of England or Church of Rome. There was nothing else."

15

They both had trays. Sable followed Harry into a relatively quiet corner of the staff canteen. He looked down at his plate. "Tomato soup. Fantastic. It reminds me of my childhood – happy days."

Sable smiled at him as she tested her thick vegetable soup. It was hot, so she stirred it gently and took small sips.

"How was your morning?" he asked.

"Pretty steady, thanks. I'm helping our British Consulate in Lyon with a job… It's a pleasant location, beside the River Rhône."

"What sort of work?"

"Commercial. There's a Secretary over there who's been in touch with me." Sable was well into her soup by now. Harry had finished his and added that it was damn good.

"Is Lyon a big city?" he asked.

"Yes. Second only to Paris. Both the Rhône and the Saône pass through it. The city looks lovely, with a large church, Notre Dame, high on a hill. Most splendid by all accounts; I'm really keen to go there one day, " she added.

He looked up. "I favour Nice and Cannes."

"We could visit all three one summer, plus Avignon." She looked at him. "We could fly down there and hire a car."

He seemed to agree. But he also wondered how many art galleries there were in Avignon. Harry also said that he had been looking for a decent drama in the West End. He suggested he buy some tickets and she agreed.

After their pleasant lunch, they took a short walk outside. Harry was always impressed by the magnitude of the Victorian buildings. Sable wondered if he would have time to see her next weekend or possibly a week later. They discussed various dates and he said he would call her. He had always phoned in the evening which had pleased her. They parted and returned to their various departments.

***

She stood outside the Old War Office Building in Whitehall. It was located on the east side. If you looked to the north you could easily see Trafalgar Square. To the south, you could see the Palace of Westminster. It was Friday and it was close to six o'clock. There were still tourists milling about admiring them. Most people were on their way home after having put in a decent effort at the end of another working week in their offices. Some were walking briskly to the nearest tube station whilst others made their way to a bus stop.

This particular young lady, standing outside the attractive building that was made of Portland Stone, was Chinese. Her name was Han Wei and she was in her twenties. She had a permanent job in Chinatown. A fit Londoner could walk there in less than thirty minutes. Han Wei was slim and attractive. Her black hair was cut in a bob and she wore well-proportioned makeup. Her full lips were a deep red. Her skin was like ivory and she painted all her nails red. She wore a lovely dark blue dress that was cut well above the knee.

One or two gentlemen passing by saw her but made no advances towards her, probably believing that she was waiting for someone special. An observer nearby, who was selling souvenirs with the *Evening Standard*, watched her as she was suddenly being escorted down Whitehall. The couple seemed very close to each other. The gentleman, who wore a dark suit, had his arm around her waist.

Han Wei realised they had passed one public house, so was there another? To her left were various statues of military commanders, all facing Whitehall. She felt tempted to ask her boyfriend where they were going. Across the road was the entrance to Downing Street, full of tight security. She then saw the building on her left.

"Here we are, Han Wei, I think you will like it," he said, smiling. They were standing at the side entrance to The Red Lion. He indicated the steep stairs in front of her and invited her to go up. He watched her climb and appreciated that she had lovely legs and nice thighs. She was wearing clear tights.

Once they were both at the top they stopped briefly to admire the photographs that were adorning the walls. He then led the way into the small restaurant and chose a table. As soon as they had sat down, Harry gave her a passionate kiss which she liked enormously. She liked to be kissed in private.

"So, my darling, how long do you have?" he asked, as he summoned the waitress.

Han Wei was quite exact. "Only about one hour, Harry. My employer at the clinic wants me back to do another hour and a half."

Harry ordered two large tomato juices and a bowl of nuts. "Well never mind, darling, any time spent with you is just wonderful." She looked up at him and smiled. He looked at the clock and realised they had just fifty-five minutes. Harry held her hand and told her how lovely she was and how much she meant to him.

He then kissed her hand and told her that he was looking to the future. She knew he worked for the government but she had forgotten that it was the Foreign Office.

When questioned about her job, she said that it was not very onerous but she did have to work long hours. She reminded him that she performed 'massage work' at the clinic. It was all carefully controlled and regulated.

Harry wanted to take her home to meet his parents. However, he knew there was a stumbling block. They were very strict and conservative and traditional and would expect him to choose a good English girl, someone who was professional. By that, they meant she had to have been university educated. It was rather like choosing between an officer and an artificer. They would expect their son to choose the former. He knew this was a problem that he would have to work on. How to get her accepted.

When they left The Red Lion, he pointed to the wooden board on the wall at the foot of the stairs. It showed the names of previous owners: ancestors of Harry's had been proprietors from 1882 to 1889. Han Wei was impressed. Harry walked her up to the north end of Whitehall where they said their goodbyes. She hugged him tight and said she wanted to see him again soon. She had an idea – why not come to the clinic some time? Good idea. He gave her a loving kiss and watched her walk back in the direction of Chinatown.

***

"We'd like to meet Harry one day." It was her father speaking. They were at the breakfast table and both Henry and Gloria thought it was time to be acquainted with Sable's boyfriend. Meeting Henri, whom they had once spoken about, would have to wait.

Sable nodded. "Yes, of course. But last night would have been a bit late: the play slightly overran." It was more of a statement than an excuse.

Henry lowered the newspaper a little. "Darling, he could come to tea one afternoon on a Saturday." He looked at Gloria, who agreed. "It would be a relaxed and easy way to meet him – not too much protocol to be observed."

When Harry next saw Sable he told her that he had had a 'performance review'. It had gone very favourably, he said. He believed he was now waiting on HR, hopefully for a promotion either within the department or to another department.

***

Harry was sitting in the office of his line manager. It had been a very useful and productive meeting. Harry had been promoted within the department due to someone else's promotion. The wheels had been turning. The line manager, Mr Murgatroyd, handed Harry a letter. Charles Murgatroyd was an affable manager who had spent all his career in the service of his country. He had seen governments come and go, worked overseas in one or two troublespots and had distinguished himself as a skilful manager. Now in his fifties, he had the appearance of a colonel, recently retired from the British Army.

"This is your letter of official appointment. Congratulations, Harold. As you can see, you have earned a good salary increase, commensurate with your increased and heavy responsibilities. How do you like chairing meetings?"

Harry looked at the letter in his lap, glancing at some of the sentences. He gave the question hardly any thought. "I'm happy with that, sir. So long as I know exactly who will be present – the people, the departments, objectives and so on."

"Quite. You'll also be going on a course. HR will be writing to you on that one. Leadership, or something. Take it seriously. We'll get you overseas for a long stint in due course. Maintaining good international relations is vital, even if we do come across one or two pariah states, and it's best not to upset them too much either. One never quite knows what the future holds." Charles Murgatroyd then went into what Harry could only describe as 'speech' mode. He told Harry how long he had been working for the government, what he thought of today's politicians and how indispensable the Civil Service was. As far as he was concerned, it ran the country – always did and always would. He then talked about the queen and monarchy, overseas visits and how indispensable our ambassadors were. "I really do hope you make it to ambassador, Harold. I think you've got all the qualities. Perhaps a posting to Eastern Europe might be good in a few years' time. Are you married or single? Well anyway, you really need to have a wife if you want to be an ambassador. She plays a pivotal role with all the entertaining, which can be quite considerable, especially around Christmas time. It's one party after another. Most wives love it. Any questions? Good."

Charles Murgatroyd stood up to signify that the meeting had drawn to a close. He held out his hand. It was back to work.

Harry stood up. "Thank you, sir." He then departed.

As he walked back to his office he realised he would have to start sorting out his personal effects. They would be sent to his new office by the beginning of the following week, according to his letter. He also started to think about a wife. Of the girls that he knew, only Sable would be suitable to act as hostess in some foreign embassy. His beauty up in Chinatown was a charming girl, fun to be with, and he was sure she would love him to bits, and vice versa. But would she really fit in with Foreign Office protocol? Was she educated enough to understand Anglo-Saxon culture, ways and means, etc? He knew it was a problem he would have to grapple with. And for example, would Charles be more comfortable meeting Sable or Han Wei? However, if he married Sable, what would happen when he was transferred overseas? Would she be willing to give up her job and career or would she settle for a life as a diplomat's wife? Harry knew that was a difficult one.

***

Three weeks later, Harry was explaining to Henry, Gloria and Sable the good fortune of his promotion. He talked about his new office location, his versatile assistant, the sort of work he had to do as chairman of certain meetings and where it could lead. His boss had indicated that a spell in Eastern Europe might prove to be a good training ground for further promotion.

Henry was nodding sagely all the time, while Gloria was constantly focused on her daughter to judge her reaction as Harry outlined his possible future.

"And will changes in foreign policy have an impact on your job at any time?" asked Henry eagerly.

Harry thought for a moment. "I think it is more likely to shift the burden of work from one corner of the globe to another one, if you get the drift. We may have more contact and communications with both China and India and less with certain Gulf States. Commerce may increase in one country and decline in another."

Henry nodded. "Yes, I see. I'm with you." He went on. "One of those Gulf States was isolated because they were sponsoring terrorism."

"That is an extreme example – and I think most of the West cut their ties with that state," Harry acknowledged.

"And how are your eastern languages, Harry? Sable says you speak a little," asked Gloria.

"Well, today I've only got a smattering of Polish, Czech and Slovakian. I'm terribly rusty and out of practice. Unless you keep them up, you soon lose them."

Sable nodded. "I think that's true with everybody."

Henry chuckled. "Even our friend Gisela almost forgot her German! It happens."

Harry then thought it was time to go. "Thank you both for a lovely afternoon. Such wonderful chocolate cake, Mrs Fairfax." He stood up.

She smiled. "Please call me Gloria. And I hope we see more of you, Harry. Sable will see you out."

Harry gave Sable a kiss before climbing into his car.

"You've got lovely parents, darling. I'll call you soon. We'll have to think about the summer."

"I do hope your job goes really well," she called.

And with that he was off.

Meanwhile, back in the lounge, Gloria was conferring with her husband on the suitability of this young man.

16

During the next week, there was a long meeting planned for the Wednesday, so Harry had to cancel his lunch date with Sable. Instead, he found time to make an appointment in Chinatown at the end of the week. After a challenging five days in the office, he looked forward to a relaxing massage.

Han Wei was delighted to see him at six thirty. He entered the cubicle and found his girl wearing a white clinical mini dress and white high heels. She threw her arms around him and they kissed passionately. He stripped down to his underpants and lay face down on the couch.

"How did you get here, darling?"

"I walked. Easiest way."

"That's good."

She then used her hand muscles to massage his neck and his shoulders. He let out a sigh of relief and told her it was wonderfully relaxing.

"I ought to send my line manager up here. Now that would be exciting." He started laughing.

Han Wei was puzzled. "Darling, what is line manager? "

He turned his head a little. "Oh, you know, a boss." He thought she understood. "By the way, what's under your dress?"

She giggled. "Darling, I'll show you in ten minutes' time." He just wished there was the same strong sexual chemistry with Sable.

***

At about the same time, a young Frenchman was making a phone call from Paris. He had had difficulty in making a connection, but eventually he got through. The person he was phoning had just arrived home. She was just about to sit down when her phone became very audible.

"I'll take it upstairs," she told her parents. Moving swiftly up to her room, she immediately knew who it was.

"Sable, it's me, ça va?" cried the unmistakeable young, but clear voice of her dear friend in Paris.

"Henri. So good to hear from you. Bon soir. Oui, ça va bien – all is well, thank you. And your parents – Brigitte, Roland?"

Henri searched for the right words. "Yes. They are well and send you their best wishes. They remember your visit so clearly."

"That is really so kind of you to say that," Sable replied. "So, what news? Are you coming to London? Love to see you."

There was a slight pause. "Sadly, no. But my father might be over soon on a short political visit. I will let you know, probably by email. He'll stay at the embassy, or something like that," Henri replied.

"Love to see you any time, Henri." She tried to sound convincing.

"Au revoir…"

Sable closed off the phone and sat down to think. She then immediately ran downstairs to tell her mother that Henri had been on the phone. Her mother was naturally pleased for her. When Sable told her that Roland might be coming over, Gloria thought they should at least try to see him, if only briefly. Also, her mother had something else on her mind. "Don't you think we ought to invite Henri sometime, just for a weekend?" her mother suggested.

Sable agreed. It was left like that.

***

Back in the office, Sable received a message from Harry to join him for lunch the following week on a day of her choosing. He would try to fit in with her.

After lunch, she went to the library to read the newspapers. She immersed herself in *The Daily Telegraph*, which she thought was one of the more reliable newspapers. The standard of journalism and English was usually better than in most of the other papers. America and Russia were dominating the foreign news. The new president seemed to be in the papers every day and occupied more space than the British prime minister.

She then remembered something that she had to look up in her French dictionary when she returned to her desk. But the future slightly bothered her. If she was to marry Harry, and they were both still in London, fine. But as soon as he was posted to an overseas embassy, she would likely have to give up her job and go as the diplomat's wife. She would be extremely lucky if they found her a job in the same embassy.

No. Sable knew she wanted to make use of her university and career training and work as a professional. She, too, wanted to rise up the secretarial ranks and become an ambassador one day. She liked the responsibility and decision-making and having polite discussions with diplomatic staff. Maintaining good international relations was vital. She wanted to be part of that global process.

Meanwhile, when it came to personal friendships and relationships, she saw this as an evolving dilemma. She consoled herself in remembering that circumstances often played a role in sorting things out.

***

An email came through from Paris two weeks later. It was from Henri. He said his father was coming over to

London to have a meeting with various ministers. He thought the Dutch prime minister was also coming.

Sable sent a text to her mother, who in turn asked her to find out the date and see if Roland would have time to pop down for a meal. Gloria noted that this was one of the disadvantages of not living in Central London. But she was sure the French would have a competent chauffeur who could find his way out of London.

Sable hoped she could avoid meeting Gerit; it could just be slightly embarrassing.

On the next day she had to attend a large meeting. It was sort of in a lecture theatre, and had the benefit of being equipped with a huge screen. The speaker, from personnel, introduced herself. She then talked about overall staffing levels within the Foreign and Commonwealth Office. She went on to describe some of the recent money-saving initiatives by the present government and how the FCO was going to try to implement them satisfactorily and painlessly.

The presenter then focused more on Europe. Hopefully this would be a little more relevant, thought Sable. Embassies and consulates came under the spotlight. To give one example, the presenter showed a slide which was a map of France. It showed sixteen locations of consulates and consulates-generals all over France. This was in addition to the embassy in the capital, situated in the rue du Faubourg Saint-Honore.

Then the spotlight changed to Germany. The FCO had closed consulates in the cities of Frankfurt and Stuttgart. The other three remained in Hamburg, Dusseldorf and Munich. The embassy, of course, was in the Wilhelmstrasse, Berlin. Overall, the talk had been quite interesting and informative.

When she was least expecting it, Sable received a message from Harry to have her bag packed next Saturday morning. It took her by surprise but, at the same time, it sounded exciting. He would collect her.

On the night before, she knew she and Harry were going to a theatre in London after work. They had a quick meal in the canteen before going to what Harry described as a 'comedy'. The seats were decent enough and, in fact, most seats had been sold out. The play had been given a modest write-up in the press, so Harry knew not to expect too much. However, the actors were quite well-known. There was plenty of laughter even if the plot was rather simple. Sable enjoyed it.

After the show, and because it was a trifle late, they agreed to part company and go straight home. Harry said he would come for her in the late morning.

Next day she was packed and ready by ten. She told her parents that they were going away for the weekend, destination unknown. She sat in the lounge with her father, waiting.

"Mystery tour, darling?" enquired Henry.

She smiled. "I just hope it's somewhere decent."

"I'm sure it won't be a caravan. Mind you, there's a lovely caravan park I read about in South Dorset, on the coast at Durdle Door. I think you have to rent them for a minimum of one week – you know, a summer holiday." Henry turned the page.

Sable nodded. She looked at the clock. Where was he?

As if by answering her question, his car arrived. Harry opened the boot and then knocked on the door. After all the usual pleasantries, Harry promised to return their daughter in one piece on Sunday.

They drove off and Harry headed in a westerly direction.

"Did you enjoy the theatre?" he asked as a car raced past, exceeding the speed limit.

"Mm. Yes thanks, Harry. It was different."

She looked around and recognised that they were heading for the M25. "Where are we going?"

"Hampshire. We'll need the A303 for a while before moving south. There's a map by your feet. But I think I know it."

As she studied the map, the weather began to improve. Harry drove at a sensible speed. He looked across and smiled as Sable started to examine the road systems leading down into Hampshire. It was always his contention that women could never understand maps, never know their north from their south, or where the sun rose and set. And he recalled a story from a school trip in Somerset in which a group of girls were driving east one summer evening. As they came over the brow of a hill they suddenly saw a huge red ball in the sky. They thought it was the sun. It was in fact the moon, carrying the sun's reflection. He was still convinced today that girls simply could not navigate.

He looked at her. Was Sable struggling with this map? He told her he was heading for the A30. She continued to study the road map with a small frown on her face. She then put the map on the floor and took out her iPad. She noticed she had new emails in. One was from May Ling and the other from Maria. She read them both with interest. May Ling was in Hong Kong, earning better money and speaking both English and German. It was part of her job. This prompted Sable, so she decided to send a short reply to May Ling and another short message to Jill Kamudona in West Africa. All this email activity reminded Harry of his passionate girl in Chinatown. With Han Wei on his mind, he nearly missed the turning to the left. He turned the wheel just in time. Shit, he said to himself.

"Sorry about that. We are now heading southwest."

She looked at him. "Salisbury? Is that it?"

He drove on. He was familiar with the road and soon they were entering the small town.

"Stockbridge? Good Lord. I don't know it," she said.

He pulled up at the Grosvenor Hotel. "This is it. It should be comfortable enough." They had a decent room overlooking the back garden, and what looked like a large comfortable double bed and a connecting bathroom.

He went up to her and put his arms round her. "Will this suit you, darling?"

She looked around and gave it her approval. "Yes, I think so." She gave him a kiss. "Kind sir. I just hope the bed's not lumpy."

"Well, time for that later. Put your shoes on and let's go for a walk. I think there's a river nearby. I might test your knowledge."

The town had only one main street. It was a wide thoroughfare, running east to west, and to the west lay Salisbury.

Harry and Sable made their way down the quaint old street. There was a mixture of both local people, plus visitors, and it was hard to tell who were in the majority. Sable was fascinated by some of the old shops – they were stepping back a century in time. This was England; this was a decent little market town in Hampshire. She was a tourist and she was going to enjoy herself.

They found a quaint shop selling antiques. Harry was fascinated by the lovely old furniture, one piece of which was a cockfighting chair. It belonged to the eighteenth century. "If it's still here in a year's time, I'll buy it," he murmured to her.

They moved on and found the river. "Oh, good Lord, the River Test. I remember that from school," she cried.

They had lunch in a nearby café. Harry said they would explore the area to the south afterwards. Luckily, the weather was holding. They went back for the car and explored the river valley. They had both forgotten how lovely Hampshire really was since their childhood days. There was the river with its lovely banks, the wildlife all around, footpaths and familiar trees. They took a short walk and, to their surprise, encountered an otter with her pups. Sable just loved it.

As dusk approached, they were back in the hotel. Harry opened up the minibar. He chose a cold beer while he poured a gin and tonic for his girl. "Darling, would you like a shower or a bath?"

She was sitting in an easy chair, sipping and savouring the gin and tonic. She smiled at him. "Let's have a soak."

He ran the bath and was soon undressed, putting on one of the white bathroom robes with its distinctive initials.

"I'll get in first and make a start."

While Harry was making masses of soapy water, Sable undressed. Before entering the bathroom, she opened up the bed to inspect it. It all appeared to be rather smart and clean. But there were far too many pillows, so she put two of them over on the far side of the room. She then turned on the radio and selected some soft music. Satisfied with the room now, she opened the door and entered the steamy bathroom.

They were soon in each other's arms, enjoying the fun of a huge bath – a new experience for both of them.

After they had ordered dinner, they laughed about several things. Firstly it was their antics in the bathroom. They had had rather a fun experience, especially when Harry started to rub down Sable and tickle her near her thighs.

Then their conversation centred on some of the other staff in the FCO. There were one or two slightly colourful characters whom they had both come across, male and female. They talked about procedure and politics, iPads and inkpads, files and folios and whether the overall pace of modernisation in the FCO was rapid enough.

Harry ordered cheese, biscuits and celery for them both instead of icecream. He also asked for two glasses of port. He favoured Taylor's.

By the time they reached the bedroom they were in high spirits. There was just time to watch the news highlights before Harry insisted they get to bed sooner rather than later.

Not wanting to risk anything, she insisted that Harry wore one of those 'things'. Reluctantly, he agreed.

"I'm not on the pill, darling, but I soon will be." He nodded, then smiled. They both realised that they were new to each other. After a bit of careful thought and consideration, Harry ended up on his back with Sable on top, applying all her skills and shear common sense.

They both knew they had a lot to learn and, quite simply, needed to practice in order to make it a joyous and fulfilling event.

Harry had set the alarm so that they could have a bath before breakfast. He got it running and told her to go first while he had a shave. She made a mental note to shave her pussy when she got back home. She also wondered why they were not making love again. Perhaps he was tired.

Afterwards, he watched the morning news while she got dressed and applied her makeup. He turned to face her. "We live on bad news, don't we?" It was fair comment.

She nodded. "Silly, isn't it."

Soon they were downstairs and ready to enjoy the buffet breakfast. The choice was almost difficult. This was the stuff for a decision-making course. They chose a table by the window. Sable chose muesli followed by a cooked meal; somehow she managed to squeeze three sausages onto her plate. Meanwhile Harry chose four yogurts, muesli, scrambled eggs, bacon, apples and bananas.

"Harry. What are you doing?" exclaimed Sable, scarcely believing what she saw.

He smiled. "Darling, after last night, well, I'm very hungry. It makes me hungry. You'd better make a note of that, please – for the future."

"Mostly at weekends then?" She smiled at him.

When Harry went to refill his coffee cup, he picked up a Sunday newspaper. They divided it in half as they ate.

Sixty minutes later they were on the road leading out of this nice little town and were heading west.

"I know this road. It's a straight run there. Dead straight – must be Roman," he commented.

They drove through cultivated fields until Sable suddenly pointed at the distant spire. "Salisbury! Look!"

Harry drove round the city until he could find a suitable parking place that was not too distant from the cathedral. Soon they had parked the car and were walking towards the building that had the tallest spire in England.

"Thirteenth century, I'd say." With that, Sable looked at Harry as if to challenge him.

"I'm sure you're correct."

They made their way inside and caught the end of a commentary for a group on a tour. They discovered the early English Gothic-style structure had an elaborate exterior, decorated with pointed arches and flying buttresses; the interior was sombre and austere. They walked round, taking in the pure magnificence of the huge edifice. In the north aisle they came across the fascinating mediaeval clock dating from 1386, and said to be the oldest working timepiece in the world.

"Oh my goodness – quite amazing," she said.

Harry and Sable were almost stunned at the amazing clock, particularly when one had to consider the professional craftsmanship involved. They almost shook their heads in disbelief at the skill and craftsmanship that went into it in those early days. They gave the cathedral a thorough viewing and when they emerged, more like new scholars than tourists, it was time for a late lunch in the old part of town. They walked down the streets, taking in a vast amount of history, much of which would probably be forgotten in a week's time.

They read that the city had been an important provincial city for more than a thousand years; its streets formed an architectural timeline, ranging from the mediaeval walls and half-timbered Tudor town houses to Georgian mansions and Victorian villas.

As they ate their lunch, consisting of sandwiches and salad, Harry contemplated his future with Sable. He thought that she would be a very suitable bride and companion. "It's been a great weekend, darling. Thank you for coming."

She looked at him. "Yes. It's been rather special. We've got on rather well, in all departments." She paused to think. "We just need to practice a little, don't we?" She let out a giggle. "It is a rather wonderful city and Winchester is not too far away, as well." She looked round. "I'm sure I came here long ago. But you don't appreciate such places when you are so young."

"That's true," he agreed.

There was a slight pause. "Darling, there's a future out there for us if we want it. I'd love to have you beside me."

She nodded, gracefully. He took her hands and squeezed them.

"All right, Harry. Take me to Winchester."

Somewhat surprised, he looked at the clock. "What, now?"

She almost kicked him. "No. Silly. Not now, but soon."

He smiled. "Yes, I see. Right." He looked at their glasses. "More wine? I need some water. I'm driving."

When he was up at the bar gathering some sparkling water, he heard a message come through. It was from Han Wei. She wanted to see him. So he took the water back to the table and disappeared to the WC.

Inside the privacy of a cubicle, he sat and read the message again. Then he made up a very sensible story and sent it back. But he knew he would see her soon. He remembered how she had taken off her white dress at the clinic and how he had been amazed at her superb figure. Her breasts were large and were barely contained within her cups. He had kissed them both. Then he had tickled her inside her thong. She was smooth, without a hint of stubble. She had whispered in his ear that she wanted to see him again really soon, outside, somewhere in London.

She told him that he was a man whom she could deeply love all her life. Those words were ringing in his ear as he walked back to Sable.

Back at their table they finished the sparkling water. Then it was her turn to disappear down the passage.

Time to go, he thought. It had been both fun and useful. She was a great girl. Don't lose sight of that fact, he told himself.

They returned to the car and were soon heading back towards the Home Counties. She continued to read parts of the newspaper while he drove at a steady pace. She did not know it but Harry had two things on his mind – Han Wei, and planning the visit to Winchester. He knew he could visit Hen Wei either at the clinic or at other carefully chosen locations in London. The trip to Winchester could be done in about six to eight weeks, he thought. Sable was going to go onto the pill so she had to allow time for it to become effective.

17

"Hello, sir. As promised, one daughter returned, safe and sound."

Henry had opened the door and was happy to see them. He helped Sable with her bag while Gloria offered Harry a drink. He declined the offer as he had to get home and was not overkeen on night driving, even at his tender age. And tomorrow was a working day at the FCO. They said their goodbyes. Sable watched his car disappear then went in.

"And did it match your expectations?" asked her mother, keen to be given chapter and verse and every minute detail.

"Oh, yes. This country has so much to offer the domestic tourist. Stockbridge is a dear little town while Salisbury is so full of hidden treasures," said Sable, full of enthusiasm. She went on to relate some of what they had done in both locations. It was the ancient clock that had stayed in her mind, apart from one or two other things.

Gloria hinted that she had never visited Salisbury. Henry said it would be an excellent place to go themselves, at which point Gloria almost jumped into Henry's lap and gave him a huge hug. Sable wondered if she and Harry might be like that one day. Also, she wondered what the hotels in Winchester were like. She might do some researching. Did all hotel rooms have a surplus of pillows?

Next day she was back at work, keen to get her mind round various problems that required her attention. It was good to be using her dictionaries again. Quite why school children had given up on them baffled her. The young kept using their pads and iPhones. 'Dictionaries were for dinosaurs' was a phrase she had once heard. To her, a dictionary was indispensable: you opened the page, saw your word but also learnt so many other words from the open two pages. A dictionary was a bonus. And some came with the thesaurus as well.

At the end of the week she had supper in town with Maria. She was her friend for life and Sable felt she could tell her anything. She always valued Maria's advice.

Sable described the weekend as sensibly as she could, highlighting valid points. She told Maria that Salisbury required at least a long weekend – there was actually quite a lot that they had not seen in depth.

"And how do you feel about Harry?" Maria asked. "Are you more enlightened?"

She nodded her head. "Oh yes. It was good to see him in a relaxed state away from the office, away from pressures of work. We got on well. We're quite close." She smiled.

"Could you love him?" Maria asked.

Sable thought about it. "Yes, I think so. He knows what he wants, and he's got a career in the FCO. That's most important."

"But, darling, is he reliable and dependable? Does he have any skeletons in the cupboard, as they say? And darling, don't forget, you also have a career in the FCO."

Sable sat there, pondering these pertinent questions. "Well, I'll try and find out when we next go away. I've told Harry that I want to visit Winchester."

"When?"

"Possibly in about a month's time, maybe six weeks. It all depends how full their hotels are. It's a very popular place with tourists, you know. I'm sure we drove through the city once but that was before the motorway was built. I've forgotten most of it. Now London dominates my life."

"That's only natural," observed Maria. "But seriously, darling, if there is someone else in his life, they're bound to keep phoning him. Just keep your ears open, unless he switches it off completely."

Sable sort of nodded her head. "Well. All right. But it may not happen."

Maria continued, on a cautionary note, "When you get to Winchester, just ask yourself if Harry makes you happy, and at the end of the weekend, ask yourself the same type of question: does he make me happy now and will he make me happy in five years' time? And have I found my stable, reliable gentleman partner for life?"

Sable was surprised. "Gosh, darling, you're very philosophical — "

Maria summed it up. "It's so very easy to get hurt. Darling, it's important."

"If he ever cheated on me, I'd kill him," said Sable in a purposeful tone.

Maria then asked the waitress for some more coffee. She also wondered if Sable needed a tranquiliser.

***

Henry and Gloria were having supper. Something was on their mind. Sable's future happiness was of paramount importance to them, naturally, but Gloria couldn't put Henri out of her mind. He sounded like a very pleasant young man.

She turned to Henry. "Darling, did I dream it or did Sable tell us that Henri's father was coming to London?"

He remembered. "Oh good Lord, yes, what was his name? Tassier?"

She looked at him. "Roland Tassier?"

"Yes, that was it. He was supposed to be coming over for a business meeting, here in London," Henry recollected. "And we were going to offer him a meal, if he could find his way here. We're supposed to be waiting on further bulletins from Sable."

"Perhaps he won't be coming. Meetings do get cancelled, you know," she said.

Henry nodded. "Quite."

***

Just to the north of Marble Arch is a lovely building that was restored from a previous building on this site and which dated from the 1920s. Part of the exterior consists of Portland Stone. Containing just over one thousand rooms, and of differing prices, it is the Cumberland Hotel. Also, just to the north and west of Marble Arch, is a lovely building with its origins in late Victorian to early Edwardian times. Part of the front façade contains sandstone brought over from France and above the doorway is a lovely flag. To the left of the main entrance was a tablet that named the house and gave the year of 1907.

But the young couple who had made their way to this part of town were just keen to be together. Admiring the local architecture was not their priority.

They were in their room in the private wing of what was a jolly splendid club. Harry was on his back, with Han Wei on top of him, her eyes closed as she let out shrieks of pure joy – this time in Mandarin.

Later, she lay on top of the man whom she desperately loved. She hugged him tight, promising never to let go.

Thirty minutes later, they were sitting up in bed enjoying a good bottle of champagne that Harry had brought with him in his luggage.

"A good way to end the week," he declared with a smile. "But I tell you, darling, I'm totally exhausted. That was some performance."

"We suit each other perfectly, darling." She finished her drink then hugged him tight. "Darling, I want to be a Foreign Office wife. An ambassador's wife. The foreign secretary will just love me, and all that I can do, to make you one of the best ambassadors in the service."

Harry was somewhat stunned and lost for words. He felt like telling her that foreign secretaries were politicians and could be replaced, or shuffled, at the whim of the prime minister. It was in her gift to change her Cabinet when she chose. But he knew that would only spoil things.

Next morning, Han Wei wore a lovely dark mini skirt and blue blouse. It was Saturday so they had time for a leisurely breakfast. While she devoured lots of yogurt, Harry picked up a discarded Saturday newspaper from the adjacent table. He wondered how much bad news there was.

"Oh, darling, I do have to be at the clinic at one today. Sorry. I've just seen it in my diary."

She was looking at her glass tablet which clearly controlled her life. In sympathy with hers, he took his own out from an inside pocket and looked for any messages. Surprisingly, there was nothing except a reminder of a meeting next week in the office. He knew about that anyway.

He looked at her. She was well made-up for work, with her eyes looking totally beautiful and not a hair out of place. If only all British girls could be like this, he thought. So many girls seemed to have long, unmanageable hair that constantly got in their eyes.

One hour later he was escorting her back by Underground to Leicester Square. She had loved every moment with him. After a passionate kiss down a small side street, she had carried her little suitcase to the clinic, where she waved him goodbye. He blew her a kiss and smiled radiantly at her. Then she was gone.

Harry took the Underground back to West London and to his home. He thought about Han Wei, he thought about Sable and then he read the foreign news in the newspaper. It appeared that the Dutch prime minister had survived a vote of no confidence. The man's name was Gerit Schmidt.

***

During the next six weeks Harry and Sable found time to visit the cinema on two evenings. Sable made the choice and Harry went along with it. They also found time to have supper on two occasions and a more formal dinner in the City, which Sable really loved.

Sable's father knew the City because he worked there but Sable knew little of the geography of the City. Her patch was Whitehall.

Harry also had to attend a conference. It was this workload that he used to explain to Han Wei why he could not see her on two specific days. She was naturally very disappointed but did not kick up too much of a fuss; she still did not know the ins and outs of Harry's job.

***

They were travelling back from Winchester where they had just spent a very happy two days and one night. It was on the Sunday, in particular, that Harry and Sable had talked about their future. She smiled as they had great plans to make.

They had both enjoyed the city of Winchester. The cathedral had obviously required an inspection but what they found much more interesting was the Great Hall and Round Table. They discovered that the Great Hall was the only part of the eleventh century Winchester Castle that Oliver Cromwell spared from destruction. The Round Table was said to be mythical and had been used by King Arthur. Both Harry and Sable recalled their school history lessons: it was now clear what their teachers had been waffling on about.

On Sunday lunchtime they had visited the Wykeham Arms, a well-known drinking spot. They both agreed that this memory might remain with them longest.

Harry was pleased that Sable was now used to the contraceptive pill; all seemed to be working well and they had spent a very passionate and fulfilling night. She had even persuaded Harry to perform before breakfast. "Thank goodness for advances in modern medicine," he declared.

When they arrived back at Sable's home, it was obvious to Gloria that something had happened.

When they sat down in the lounge, Sable proudly displayed her engagement ring to her parents. And Harry asked Henry if he could marry his daughter.

Henry looked at his wife and then stood up. "Well congratulations, young man. If you can promise me that you'll stay in the Foreign Office and give it all you've got, then yes, I think Gloria and I will be most happy to agree. But please don't forget one thing, my daughter is also ambitious." At that point he smiled at Harry and shook him warmly by the hand. Sable went over to hug her mother.

"Have you time for a drink – or are you driving?" Henry asked. Before they could answer, he said, "I know. I'll open that other bottle and we'll all have just half a glass, and then another bottle another time."

While Henry was assembling it all on a tray, Gloria examined the ring, which sat well on Sable's finger. The sapphire colour was ideal. Gloria approved.

When everyone had a glass, Henry and Gloria stood up and drank the health of the happy couple. It was smiles all round. The conversation then centred on all the usual preparations but also on where they might think of living. Harry took the lead and said that they would be looking at a church wedding and finding a house to live, somewhere in the west or southwest. A good commuter line was essential. He knew of the various routes into Waterloo and the range of the Underground. Where they chose to live might be determined by house prices. They could always start off by renting, if necessary.

"And are you staying in London for the time being, Harry?" Henry asked.

"I believe so, yes. I'm in a new position now and it will be up to my line manager as to when I go overseas."

Sable looked at her fiancé and nodded her approval.

After Harry had departed, Sable sat down with her parents. She looked a trifle tired so her mother recommended she have an early night.

When Henry and Gloria were in bed, she brought up the subject of Henri and realised that they might never see him. Henry tried to look at things pragmatically.

"Darling, if he came over, he would have to find a job. And don't forget, he's French and not British, and what would happen then: get him into the Foreign Office? It might not be so easy. Find a job elsewhere in

177

London? It might be difficult. Don't you think it's best for our daughter to have an English husband?

Gloria reluctantly agreed.

***

"Darling, that sounds wonderful! When's it going to be?"

Maria was so excited for her dear friend, especially when Sable appointed her as principal bridesmaid.

"Won't you need two?"

"There's plenty of time to find another, if we need to," answered Sable, who then went on to tell her that she and her parents would have to choose the church and try to fix a date.

Maria was always very supportive. "It sounds as if you have found a good man."

Sable laughed. "No, he's just found a very good and reliable girl." At which point they both laughed and promised to see each other soon. Dinner with her parents was suggested.

18

Harry and Sable started looking for properties on the internet, in local papers as well as in the *Evening Standard* and also by visiting their reputable local offices. It was a time consuming business, but in spite of this, there wasn't a huge amount for sale in their price range.

On some weekends they searched and viewed on their own, while at other times they went together and had the benefit of a stronger and more critical approach. They had been to various mortgage lenders and, being a couple, had the benefit of their two salaries combined. Their borrowing potential was quite high yet they still had to continue saving hard for their deposit. They really wanted a small 'semi' if they could find it. Harry favoured an old property with large rooms but Sable wanted something a little more modern; a small garden or patio was also essential for dining outside in summer. At least they had agreed on that.

After a fraught exchange one evening on the phone with Harry, her mother advised her that compromises were an essential element of a good and sound marriage. Gloria also said there had to be plenty of 'give and take'.

"Darling, one has to be flexible and tolerant," cautioned her mother.

Sable realised there was so much to learn. And at supper one evening, Henry almost went into the legal side rather deeply.

"Darling, it's a marriage contract but at the same time there are two of you and it is a loving partnership. You agree to clauses and you make promises." Henry tried not to sound as if he was giving a lecture or pleading in a courtroom. "You also put your wealth on the table and it becomes your joint wealth or your 'commonwealth' so to speak. It's half and half."

As she lay in bed that night she hoped that Harry would be just as flexible as she would have to be, and still look after his partner. Sable then remembered that famous divorce case that she had read about in the newspaper where an ex-wife was claiming simply vast sums of money. How hideous the world could be at times, she thought.

But there was something else that she did not know. Harry had not severed his links to Han Wei. But he was trying to convert his liaison with her from that of lover to close friend. He was seeing her less and less, firmly putting the blame on pressure of work. On one evening after work, he took some flowers to the clinic and deposited them at reception with strict instructions that they give them to Han Wei. He made the excuse that he was required back in Whitehall, which had actually been true two nights ago. There had been a bit of a flap on.

Five days later Harry had woken with a very stiff neck. He knew he had slept in an awkward position. He struggled in to work and only gradually did the pain subside. He phoned Han Wei and asked for an appointment either in the afternoon or in the evening. He explained the problem.

At six in the evening, Han Wei was helping Harry remove his shirt. She then helped him secure a comfortable position on the bed.

"Embrocation and heat is what you need, darling. But it may be a nerve that you have caught."

That was perhaps some consolation to Harry. She said it could have been worse. She then told him to go home and wrap a hot towel round his neck. She helped him on with his jacket. "Poor darling, come back if it continues."

Harry went home to find that hot towel.

Many months later, Sable and Harry knew they would probably have to rent a house or flat first of all. It would be logical to try to rent in the area in which they hoped to purchase.

***

Charles Murgatroyd was generally impressed that Harry had got himself engaged to 'one of the girls down the other end of the building', as he put it. He was also pleased that Harry's fiancée was an excellent European linguist.

"You've got to marry someone professional, dear boy, otherwise there's a bit of an imbalance," advised Charles. "Especially when you work overseas in a senior position."

"I see, yes sir," said Harry.

"By the way, when is that seminar that you're attending? And by all accounts, the job's going well, I hear?"

Harry explained that he was away for two days next week. Charles wished him a pleasant and constructive time.

Harry was still nursing a sore neck but it was gradually improving. It was not affecting his job too much as he was able to delegate. And by the time of the seminar he might be so much better.

On the following Monday, Harry made his way to the hotel where the seminar was being held. His briefing notes informed him that there would be staff from a number of departments, with most of them coming from the Home Office and the Foreign Office. The hotel was equipped with large conference suites. Their timetable showed that the first day was mainly devoted to lectures and mini-presentations. There were also lectures on government policy through the ages together with a history of foreign policy on Europe. To make sure everyone got to know each other, and to assist with interdepartmental cooperation, they were all having dinner together in the hotel and were staying the night. Apart from anything else, it would be a useful exercise in communication.

In their dining room they were to sit at large round tables; in addition, there was a seating plan. Seated near to him on his right was an Eastern European girl who had become naturalised in Britain. She was a member of staff in the Home Office. Harry noticed that she had her black hair in a sort of bob, wore red lipstick and was generally rather striking to look at. When Harry caught her eyes, she smiled radiantly at him. He was surprised but not unhappy. He politely returned the smile and noticed that she was wearing a navy blue jacket. It suited her.

During the meal, Harry chatted to the people to his left and right. Much of the time they discussed government policies and how they were going to implement them. All sorts of problem areas were discussed. Harry enjoyed getting to grips with possible solutions. Only on two occasions did Harry make further eye contact with the girl. She seemed happy enough.

It was over coffee that Katia came over and introduced herself. She had noticed that the chair to Harry's right had been abandoned, so she took the initiative and sat on it. In the narrow space between their chairs she extended her hand to Harry.

"I'm Katia Margovitch. I'm pleased to meet you," she said with a broad smile.

"Harold Jones – Foreign Office. Tell me, are you gaining knowledge from today?"

"Why yes, it's most informative. By the way, I'm originally from Eastern Europe. Now in the Home Office."

For a moment they looked at each other, perhaps captivated by looks or just plain interest.

"Tell me, Mr Jones, do you speak any eastern languages? I'm curious to know," she asked.

Harry recalled those days. "Some Polish and some Slovakian, and a tiny bit of Arabic but I am what we call 'rusty'. I just do not have the chance to practice here in London. But I do a little translation now and again. It hasn't all gone." He looked at her with an appreciative smile, "Please, do call me Harry – most people do."

Katia fully understood. "That is good."

Soon they had finished their coffee. She then looked at her watch and recommended that they retire.

"Harry, why not join me for a nightcap – there's a free minibar in the room. A shame to waste it."

This girl was a business girl, rather forward but she knew what she wanted. She was decisive, not a bad asset to have in the Civil Service where talent was always needed, thought Harry.

"All right. I'd love to."

As they walked to the lifts, he asked her if she had her room key. "Hardly a key, but I know what you mean. Are we all on the same floor? I doubt it." They stopped on the third floor and walked out. Harry followed her, walking in the slipstream of her strong perfume. It rather surprised him that she would wear it on a training course.

They entered her room and she invited him to sit on one of the two chairs. She then put on some music and went to the minibar. "What would you like, Harry? It's either beer or spirits or plenty of soft drinks."

"I'd like a beer, please."

All the single rooms were very similar in layout but the view from the windows would vary from floor to floor. Harry would have to wait until morning to see what he was looking out onto. Katia gave him his beer and she turned her chair round a little so they could talk a little more easily. She appeared to have a gin and tonic in her hand.

"Cheers, Harry. So what have you thought of this course so far?"

He thought for a moment. "Well, it's been constructive. The lectures were very relevant, I mean not everybody has a huge amount of knowledge of modern History or of British foreign policy, past and present or, indeed, of international relations. Many of us are linguists or have taken joint honours and mixed a subject with one language." Harry drank half his glass and hoped it would displace the coffee, which often kept him awake at night. "Tell me, Katia, what did you read at university?"

"I actually read law here in England. I also have Eastern European language skills which the Home Office thought would be useful."

"Yes, indeed, especially with so much immigration."

"Exactly."

Harry finished his beer. Katia immediately went to the minibar to get him a refill, and at the same time she pulled out another can of gin and tonic.

"Gosh, I really shouldn't, Katia. We've got to be on best behaviour tomorrow at eight thirty – and we've got exercises to do. Remember?"

She smiled at him. As she crossed her legs again, Harry noticed that she was wearing stockings. He tried to recall if he had ever seen Sable wearing stockings. He might buy her some.

"Harry, may I ask you a personal question?" By way of a gesture, he indicated 'yes'. "Are you married?" She looked at him with beautiful, but piercing eyes.

"No, not yet. But I am engaged."

She smiled. "Well that is just wonderful, Harry. Is she British? Oh, I'm single, by the way."

Harry smiled. "Oh yes, white Anglo-Saxon and very English. Her father's a solicitor in the City, you know, somewhere near the Bank of England."

"Ah – so that area is the City? I keep hearing it," she said, pleased that she had learnt something useful, even at this late hour.

Harry expanded, "It's the oldest administrative part of London and goes back to Roman times. It embraces St. Paul's, the Stock Exchange, the Bank, Lloyds of London and many other notable institutions. You must visit the Royal Exchange one day, Katia, after work. Go there for a drink. It's next door to the Bank of England. It's so old and fascinating."

Katia then changed the subject, as Harry carefully looked at the time. "Have you been posted overseas yet, Harry?"

"No. But I have been promoted and my line manager, as they say, hopes to send me to Eastern Europe in the not-too-distant future, as we say. No, I'm still getting used to my new job where I have to chair a lot of meetings. It's early days."

She nodded her total approval. "Quite. And well done."

He drank the remains of his beer then looked at her, in a friendly yet professional way.

"We have to work tomorrow, Katia; I think I ought to let you get your beauty sleep." He rose to go. She suddenly looked less happy, as if she wanted the conversation to extend all night. She admired Harry. She liked to think she might work for him one day.

She stood up. "Shall we have breakfast together?"

"Um, now that is a good idea. I'd love to. I'll collect you at seven thirty." Harry took out his key and knew he was on the floor above. "Easy, I'll walk upstairs to my room." She took him to the door and wished him goodnight.

As Harry walked to his room he thought about Katia. If she ever wanted to transfer to the Foreign Office, she might well make an excellent Secretary. She was not afraid of asking questions yet she remained polite. And they were both complete strangers. They could continue their conversation over breakfast.

19

While Harry and Katia were members of a team, doing their best to solve a problem that had been set by their new lecturer, Sable was in her office. She was dealing with a normal workload. Sable knew that Harry's phone was off because he was on the residential training course. But still, it would have been good to have had a brief conversation with him. Perhaps he really was too busy.

In her spare time, she and her mother had been choosing the right sort of wedding dress and something for Maria. Gloria reminded Sable to ask Harry to appoint two ushers for the church wedding.

Meanwhile Katia had taken control of one of the problems and was clearly making the most of her hidden leadership skills. The lecturer had also noticed this and was really pleased to see hidden talents coming to the fore. This was one of the purposes of a training course. Harry had also been impressed. Clearly the Home Office had an excellent member of staff in Katia.

Harry and Katia had spent a most enjoyable breakfast together. They had talked about various overseas countries, especially in Eastern Europe: the old

Soviet-controlled satellite states of the East and the hardship that the population had endured.

Harry was surprised to see Katia eat so much. She just loved cooked English breakfasts and this was after two bowls of muesli. She had also drunk four glasses of pineapple juice. Harry just did not know where she put it because she was very slim and shapely.

At the end of the training course they had to fill out the usual questionnaire. They did it the old-fashioned way on paper. Harry was generous and awarded the training company five stars. Harry and Katia also exchanged business email addresses. When it was over, Harry and Katia, and a few others with whom they had worked, all met near the front door to say their goodbyes. They all agreed it had been useful and productive. They hoped they might see glimpses of each other again. The team work had been good. And so they went in their various directions across London.

As soon as he could, Harry phoned Sable and gave her a potted version of the course. He told her how much he had liked it. She realised that his mind had been clearly focused on his work and not much else.

A couple of days later, Harry was in Charles Murgatroyd's office giving him a clear and concise account of the course.

"So it went well, Harold?"

"Yes, sir. Money well spent on this occasion. It was well organised and well conducted."

Charles sat back and took it all in. He asked a few more questions before coming to the main point. He referred to a bundle of papers on his desk. "Harold, I want you to go to our embassy in Budapest. Three days should do it. If you need more, let me know. I want your opinion on how efficient it is: you know, the secretariat, local support staff etc. As you know, we've cut back in Germany, now we need to make savings elsewhere. Can you go fairly soon?"

Harry thought for just a few seconds. "Yes, sir. Pleased to help. There's currently nothing urgent in my diary at the moment. What sort of work do they cover?"

"Well, current policy, defence issues, security, trade and British exports and investment. We just need an external pair of eyes. Our ambassador will be fully cooperative. We've got a Cultural Attaché as well as a Military Attaché, but the latter is on the MoD budget."

Harry nodded. "I see. No problem."

"Good. I'll get my secretary to organise your travel and you'll stay at the Residence. They usually have one or two guest rooms."

"Fine." Harry stood up. "Thank you, sir."

As Harry walked back to his office, a few thoughts passed through his mind. He would have to tell Sable fairly soon but he then thought about Han Wei. He also wished he could take Katia with him. He was convinced that she would be excellent as an external auditor; it had become apparent during some of the exercises on the second day of their training course. She was astute and sharp. Still, there was precious little he could do about it. He would just have to do a good job himself. Even if he took Han Wei, she would have to stay in an hotel and he would never see her, except after work.

He reached his desk and looked at his diary. He made a note to phone Sable that evening and he wondered when he would be flying. Also, he noted he had several meetings in the next seven days which would keep him occupied.

Gloria had spent a busy afternoon putting together what she thought would be the bare bones of a guest list. They were also hoping to see Harry's parents again; she reflected that it was incredibly sad that his mother was confined to a wheelchair.

Gloria and Henry had spent hours on various websites trying to choose a decent caterer. They had found two in the local paper as well. After another phone call, they settled on one of the locals. At least there would be no price increase.

Soon after Sable came home, she had to excuse herself – Harry was on the line. She went upstairs and they talked for almost an hour. When she was back in the lounge her mother had a question. "Everything all right, darling?"

Sable slumped down into a chair. "Harry's going to Budapest very soon. He said he would be away for about a week – leaving me to continue to look for a property."

"Darling, don't worry. Just take it in your stride," commented her father, who took his nose out of the *Financial Times*.

Gloria then handed a piece of typed paper to Sable. "Darling, this is a skeleton guest list. Have a look at it and please add to it. But we must keep the numbers manageable. I'm sure you understand."

Sable looked at the list. She would dearly love to have put down the names of May Ling and Jill Kamudona, her dear friends from Berlin. It would have been a hell of a long journey for both. She decided she would skype them instead nearer the time. She also wondered if she ought to put Henri's name down – her dear friend in Paris. She did so as it was both polite and sensible; he could come over on the Eurostar. She then took the list upstairs to her desk, in case anyone else came into her head.

***

In Budapest, Harry spent his first day checking to see if he had all the job descriptions of staff below the more senior level. The ambassador recognised that London was looking at the staff on the middle to lower rungs of the ladder, or those in certain job groups. It would also include the local staff that the embassy had hired.

The grey-white building in Leopoldtown was quite large and square. It had several floors so Harry made use of the stairs in order to get exercise to discover the general layout of where staff were situated. One of the local women brought him afternoon tea as he was noting down names and functions. Harry needed to read all the job descriptions carefully and check to see if there was any duplication of effort. He also had a plan of personnel and departments and that gave him a clue of who did what and which section head they reported to. He also needed to read some of the email traffic.

The local woman in front of him was called Sofia. She had a lovely, friendly smile and brown hair. She wore a jacket and skirt and medium-high heels. Harry guessed that she was around forty.

"Are you settling in, Mr Jones?" she asked. "Oh by the way, there's a little kitchen on this floor and there may just be a few biscuits in the tin if you wish?"

Harry put down his pen. "Why that's very kind of you. Why not?"

She led the way. It was just round a few corners.

"And where do you work, Sofia?"

She pointed. "Just down there on the right. There are three of us in our room."

Harry put a biscuit onto a saucer and followed her to her door. Inside, there were two other staff members. One was busy typing, while the other one appeared to be sorting through some paperwork. They were both younger girls. One of them was about to stand up but Harry quickly said it was not at all necessary – nevertheless he thanked her and noted her correct manners. He was impressed.

"If I could just have your three surnames, I can then link them into one of my departmental diagrams and chain of command."

"Of course," replied Sofia. She took a pad and wrote the full names of all staff members in their department and length of service with Her Majesty's Government. Harry thanked Sofia, and wished them a happy afternoon. Equipped with the list, and his precious biscuit, he returned to his desk. The name he would remember would be Danovich, Sofia Danovich.

Before sitting down, he looked out of the window at the wide street below. He tried to imagine what it must have been like in 1956 during the Uprising. There would have been Soviet tanks on the streets. His mind then turned to the Occupation under the German Army during the 1940s. Both times would have been sheer hell for the population, especially for the Jews. He sat down, grateful that he had been lucky to have been born during peacetime.

He spent the rest of the day examining flow charts, diagrams and job descriptions of people in the same department.

Just before five, Sofia put her head round his door and knocked. Harry looked up. Sofia smiled at him. "Mr Jones, we generally go at this time. Is someone coming for you?"

Harry tried to recall a name but forgot. "Yes, I think the ambassador said his secretary would come for me and take me down." He smiled back at her.

"Then I'll see you tomorrow, Mr Jones."

As Sofia was departing, Harry forgot to remind her that she should call him Harry. He would tell her in the morning. He then put all his paperwork into his attaché case and waited for the secretary. He would do some work in his guest room.

The ambassador took him out to dinner. It was a good opportunity to talk in a relaxed setting, not just about Harry's immediate task but also about London, politics and the general economic climate.

"Things are pretty stable in this neck of the woods now. But there must have been a massive amount of tension during the Cold War. With the Berlin Wall coming down and the merging of the two Germanys, there was a brighter future to look forward to." Harry wondered, "Even today, with Putin?"

The ambassador conceded that Russia would always be an uncertain country. They agreed that it was damn hard to guess what Putin might try next.

"At least NATO is holding together," said the ambassador. "And how is our secretary of state?"

Harry shifted slightly in his seat and smiled gently. "Still bumbling along – I think."

The ambassador refilled their glasses and they had a good, but polite, laugh. "How's the job going?"

"I've got some papers to read tonight; then I need to read some email traffic in some of the departments," Harry replied.

The ambassador was very helpful. "Just shout if you need anything. My secretary is at your disposal on this."

Harry nodded. Later, he sent an email to Sable.

On his penultimate day, which was sunny after early morning rain, Sofia knocked at Harry's door.

"Good morning, Harry. I've brought you a coffee. It's rather hot."

He turned. "Why, thank you, Sofia."

She coughed very gently. "And by the way, if you would like to taste some traditional Hungarian food this evening, I am happy to invite you out. My place is not far. But only if you can spare the time. You may be too busy?" She smiled at him.

He looked at her. "That's incredibly kind of you. Will your husband be at home, or family?"

"I'm single," she said in a very slightly mournful tone.

"Well, so am I, actually... What time?"

"Shall we say five thirty. That will give both of us a full day in the office. I'll come along and collect you," she suggested.

Harry looked at the progress he had made so far and his business plan for today. He turned to her. "Yes, that should be fine. Thank you, Sofiia. See you later."

Harry used the help of the secretary to gather some email traffic twice during the day and told the secretary where he would be that evening. She said that was absolutely fine because the ambassador was out on business that evening with his wife. Harry was confident he could conclude things next day.

It was only at the end of the day that Harry was able to appreciate the different skirt and jacket that Sofiia was wearing. It was a black and white check and she had good legs under it. Perhaps she went skiing in winter, he thought.

They took a tram. "We used to have trams and trolley-buses in London once."

Sofia was surprised. "Really?"

"Now we have pollution instead."

She looked at him. She liked him. Then she heard the bell. "We're nearly there."

"Are your parents still alive?" he asked.

"My mother lives nearby, but my father was caught by the Soviets and hanged. They thought he was an agitator. They got the wrong man. Bastards."

Once outside, it was a short walk to her apartment, as she called it. "You have 'flats' in England, don't you?"

He nodded.

Once inside her modest apartment, she offered him the armchair and gave him a cold beer from the fridge. She then put on her apron and set to work. "Do you understand Hungarian? Put the TV on, there might be news."

Harry fumbled with the handset and eventually got a local programme. He struggled with the language. He then moved channels and got some international news.

The pictures of the American president said it all. He then saw a picture of the British prime minister. Hooray, he thought.

When they sat down she put a bowl of Hungarian vegetable soup in front of him.It was piping hot.

"Harry, I want to say something. I haven't got you here because I'm equivalent to a 'desperate housewife'. I just thought it would be good to chat, over my trifle and some good local tasty cheese, after you've got through that. I made it recently." She was proud of her culinary skills, which her mother had taught her.

Harry was sipping tiny spoonfuls. "This is ten times better than The Ritz."

She laughed. "Perhaps I should sell it to them?"

She told him about her job and how she had been recruited as local staff. He was really pleased for her. As a single person, she needed to have a stable position somewhere in town.

He described the size of the Foreign Office to her and its famous location; he assumed she had seen pictures of it on the internet. It was while he was trying out some of the lovely cheeses that he gave her a brief outline of some of his duties, the location of the prime minister and Cabinet and its proximity to the House of Commons.

When he looked at his watch he realised that he might be late getting back into the residence.

"You can stay here, Harry. I have a spare single room and you get breakfast with it, if you care to?

Otherwise I'll have to give you the tram number and which stop to look out for."

Harry thought there was no harm done if he stayed. If asked, he would tell the ambassador the truth.

Harry woke next morning to the smell of cooking. She knocked on his door and called out that his meal was on the table. Luckily, he had been up for thirty minutes. When he emerged he found huge cooked sausages and mushrooms on his plate. He could hardly believe it. She sat down opposite him, to yogurt and fruit.

"So, dear Harry, are you rested?"

He told her that he had slept very well. But he just did not know how to thank her for cooking yet another meal. At the very least, she deserved a free trip to London for doing all this.

She took him into the embassy and they parted near his office. He said he would come and see her before he departed. He gave her his business email address.

When Harry met the ambassador he was pleased to announce that the embassy was in very good shape. The only areas of duplication were, as far as he could see, in the Trade and Commerce department. There was some overlap which was unnecessary; two members of staff were doing the job which was largely the province of one person. That one person would have to work a little faster.

"Glad you spotted it," said the ambassador, with a genuine smile of appreciation.

"We'll need to tell London."

"Yes, I'll be informing my boss when I see him," added Harry. "If I'm done, I'll take the afternoon plane."

"Yes, of course. I'll get my secretary to book a car for you. Why not join me for lunch?"

After a reasonable meal, and farewells, Harry returned to his office to pack his things. He then went to find Sofia. The girls said she might be in the kitchen, so he retraced his steps.

"So here you are, my dear. I've come to say farewell and to thank you again."

She was looking just as charming but a little unhappy. She put her mug down and suddenly gave him a hug. "Must you go, Harry? I've so enjoyed meeting you and our time together." Tears were forming in her eyes. He offered her a tissue. He knew this would be difficult.   He did some quick thinking. "Let's stay in touch by email, Sofia. I, too, have greatly enjoyed our time together. You are charming. Perhaps you could come to London?"

She forced a smile. "Harry, I'm only local staff, not Foreign Office out of London, like you."

He gave her a hug and a kiss on the cheek. "It's been so nice. We got on so well and your hospitality was just wonderful. And we behaved."

Sofia then gave him a huge, tight hug of affection. "Harry, do you have to go today? Can't you go tomorrow? Come to my place tonight… There's masses of soup."

A smile grew across his face. Then he was serious. "Look, my darling, I'd love to but I've got a plane ticket for today – it's not open return. Supposing tomorrow's flights are all fully booked? What would my boss say? By the way, do any of you ever go on training courses – to London?" Her face said 'no'. "I'll happily pay for you to come, Sofia. But I must go today. It's expected of me. You know that." He took her in his arms and kissed her. "Do take care of yourself, Sofia. I'll be thinking of you, darling."

"As will I, Harry."

They parted. She went back to her office, completely forgetting her mug of tea.Quickly retracing her steps to the kitchen, she was so sorry that her lovely man had gone.

A few hours later, Harry's plane had started its descent to Heathrow. He had totally forgotten about Sable or indeed anything else. Once he was back in the office he would email Sofia and get her phone number at home – that would be sensible. A thought crossed his mind: did 'out of sight, out of mind' apply to everybody? Sofia had pushed literally everyone out of his mind, including Han Wei.

***

Once he was back home, Harry telephoned his parents to give them a brief account of his working visit. They were pleased for him. He couldn't face telephoning anybody else so he waited until he was back in office mode, so to speak. He thought only briefly about Sable and how her house-hunting progress had gone.

Once back in the office he was required to have meetings, firstly with Charles Murgatroyd and then with personnel, as he still called them. Charles was pleased that the visit had been constructive and had actually shown something up. Charles put it down as a successful audit. He then sat back in his chair and went into speech mode. Charles talked about the unfortunate history of the Magyar Republic, the Austro-Hungarian Empire, the Fall of Eagles, the interwar years and then the invasion of Hungary by the German Army. He rounded it off by talking about the Hungarian Uprising.

Harry stood still obediently as Charles ended his speech – yet again. "A bit before your time, dear boy. But at least you got there and back safely. Did you meet anyone nice? Now then, when are you meeting with personnel?"

Harry opened his diary. "The day after tomorrow. And yes, the ambassador is a very approachable person."

"Good. So he should be. OK. That's all. Back to work Harold. Well done."

Harry returned to his desk to resume his normal duties; there were masses of papers and letters in his In-tray. He eased himself back into his chair to think, and all he could think of was Sofia.

20

Ten minutes later he had sent his email to Sofia. He told her the journey had gone well and that he had delivered his report, now that he was back in the office.

He sent a message to Sable, suggesting they meet at the next weekend. Poor Han Wei would have to wait.

Unable to think very clearly, Harry drew a sketch and wrote down the names of the two girls in his life. He then listed all the problem areas with them both, where to live, advantages, disadvantages, and likely pathways into the future, based on his career prospects. While he was writing and thinking, one or two people came into his office to consult him. He dealt with them as quickly as he could.

Unwilling to push Sofia out of his mind, he knew he had to see Sable and see how things were going. Would they still feel close?

When he met up with Sable at the weekend, she was really pleased to see him. She took him by the arm and showed him the flat that they were going to start their married life in. They would be renting until they could find their ideal semi. In the meantime, she reminded him that they would be living apart until married. Her father was a very traditional person. The photographs of the flat showed it to have two double bedrooms. Harry sat there, taking it all in. He admired Sable for all the hard work that she had done in his absence.

"And did you see anything of Budapest?" she asked.

"Not really. If I had had the time, I would have visited the Hotel Gellert; they have excellent Turkish baths."

"Another time. Now don't forget, darling, it's only a few weeks away, our big day. Everything is booked. And have you booked the hotel?" She looked at him seriously.

He thought. "Er, yes," he said, knowing full well that he had forgotten all about it. It was a hotel in Hampshire. He reminded himself to phone them when he was at home. He also phoned the best man for a chat.

She told him that she and her mother had been so very busy. Harry then said he had some work to do but promised to be at her home for supper. Maria would be there; she was the principal bridesmaid.

Harry phoned the hotel and booked the first night. He then tried to call Sofia – she appeared to be out.

That night, Harry enjoyed a convivial supper with Henry and Gloria. He had met Maria before but only briefly. She was a bit like your typical public school girl. Everything good was all 'jolly hockey sticks'.

Maria wanted to learn more about Hungary. Harry carefully told her that he had not been a recent tourist so her best bet was either the internet or a good encyclopaedia. But he did tell her that they had trams, in common with many European cities.

Sable reminded Harry to book two weeks' holiday, to commence after the wedding. He would notify Charles and remind him.

When he arrived home, Harry discovered that Sofia had left a message on his landline. There was also an email from Han Wei – she wanted to learn all about his time away.

During the next few weeks at the office, Harry was chairing some meetings and tying up loose ends. He told his assistant to hold the fort during his absence. He had also booked his morning clothes. He had been given details of some of the guests but had not actually seen the guest list. No doubt there would be a large number of people whom he had never heard of, and would probably never see again.

***

The big day had arrived. Everybody was up early, especially Maria, who knew it would be sensible to have a large breakfast. The next meal would be a long way off. She looked at the clock. It was time to buy a newspaper. As she walked to the shop she looked up at the clouds and decided it was definitely going to stay dry this Saturday.

It was when she was walking back, scanning the headlines, that she nearly missed him. She was very close to her flat when she happened to turn her head and heard a woman's voice. Maria stopped to look. What she saw almost shocked her: a youngish woman, wearing very little and leaning out of the window, was waving goodbye to her boyfriend. The words had been unmistakeable, spoken in a sort of Asian accent. And the young woman, attractive enough, was barely hiding her breasts.

"Bye, darling, see you soon." He waved, called out goodbye and turned the other way. But it was enough for Maria to get the shock of her life when she recognised him as Harry.

He turned and walked briskly to his car. She knew the car because she had seen it at Henry and Gloria's house. He got in and drove away quickly.

Meanwhile, up in the room, the woman had stayed at the window as she watched the car drive away.

Harry! Maria had seen Harry – and he was getting married today! So what the hell was he doing in that flat? And who the hell was she? Maria stood still and pinched herself to convince herself that this was not some silly dream.

The young woman had pulled herself back into the room, breasts and all her black hair and had closed the window.

Maria walked briskly back to her flat and went into the kitchen. This was serious. She sat down to think. If it had not been for the car, she might have thought that he was some sort of lookalike, and it was not Harry at all. But no, it was him. And who was that girl? Was she a tart or somebody else? Maria thought the girl in the window had all the makings of a tart; nobody would show their breasts like that, in London! Maria nodded to herself. Yes, the young woman looked more Chinese than Japanese.

Right. She looked at the clock. Time to ring Sable.

Maria related the entire sequence of events to Sable, who had finished her bath and had just about finished drying herself. She wore her bathrobe. She was just about to use the hairdryer when her phone rang. She was not expecting any calls but when she saw it was Maria, she was happy enough.

After hearing what Maria had to say, there was a long silence.

"Darling, are you there?" Maria was very worried.

Sable replied, "Yes, yes. I'm thinking. Trying to take this in, and thinking. And you are quite sure, darling?"

"Sable, I'm as stunned as you are. It was Harry," replied Maria in a firm tone.

There was a pause. Sable had a plan. "Right, we carry on. There has to be an explanation. We'll get that later on. Some of the guests will be travelling and we can't stop things. I know my parents will agree. Come over soon, darling, as planned. Your dress is here."

"Darling, are you sure?" asked Maria.

"Yes, I think there's only one way to get to the truth."

Sable sat on her bed, finishing off her hair. All sorts of things were going through her head.

A few hours later they were all assembled with Henry and Gloria. The hairdresser had done a wonderful job for both Sable and Maria, while Gloria had looked after her own hair. Henry had to admit that his wife still looked magnificent. Henry looked at them all and then at the clock. "Well, we've got a little bit of time. Is everything in order? Anything forgotten?" He looked at them all. They were all going to go to the church in Henry's car.

Maria looked slightly nervously at Sable, wondering if she was going to say anything. Sable stood her ground and appeared confident.

Gloria moved forward. "Come on everybody, we're all going to have a tiny fruit cocktail just to keep us going until the reception."

They all sat down. As Maria nibbled at her grapefruit she wondered what on earth was going to happen. She knew she would just have to trust her best friend.

They arrived at the church with some time to spare. The car park had filled up and Henry hoped all the guests had arrived. Then suddenly a taxi turned up, and a couple climbed out. "We came by train – glad we made it on time. See you soon, old boy,"said the man, beaming widely. He just loved weddings.

Henry and Gloria waved and smiled at them – old friends.

The couple entered the church and were attended to by the ushers. Maria kept wondering, nervously. Sable then went up to Maria and gave her an instruction. Maria nodded and went into the church.

Sable turned to her father. "Daddy, we think something strange has taken place. I'm just waiting for Maria to come back. Something odd may have happened."

Henry and Gloria looked at each other. "What do you mean?" asked Henry.

"I'll tell you in a moment, Daddy."

Maria returned with news that Harry was up at the front with his parents. She then scanned the car park and could just about identify Harry's car. She pointed.

Sable turned to her father. "I suggest Mummy takes her seat. We'll follow up, but once at the top I do want to ask a question or two – it's about Harry." Henry nodded, unsure what she meant.

The procession took place and everyone stood as Sable was escorted up the aisle with her father. Maria was close behind. Eventually the organ music stopped. The vicar was just about to open his mouth when Sable interrupted proceedings.

"Excuse me, vicar, but may I ask a question?"

Unsure what the bride meant, he was somewhat at a loss and simply made a small welcoming gesture.

Sable looked at Harry in a very business-like way. "Harry, would you like to tell us all where you were last night?"

Members of the congregation started to look at one another. This was a trifle odd. Being caught off-guard, Harry recomposed himself, "I was at home."

Sable nodded, thinking. "And where were you at eight this morning?"

"The same, at home."

Sable looked at his parents for confirmation. "Is that so, Mrs Jones? Are you able to help – confirm or otherwise?"

Looking confused, Mrs Jones simply said, "Well, I didn't actually hear Harry come in. But what is this?"

Sable continued, "And Harry, I will repeat my question, where were you around eight this morning?"

"I've just told you." He looked annoyed for the first time.

Sable turned to Maria. She would ask the questions now. "Harry, what were you doing in West London this morning at eight? And who was that Chinese girl up at the window, displaying all, and waving you goodbye?"

There was real consternation and a buzzing amongst the congregation, following that last question. Some people even gasped.

Harry was silent. Maria continued, "Harry, I was there. I saw you wave her goodbye and then you walked to your car. I know your car because I have seen it at Henry's. What have you got to say?"

Harry turned to his parents. "I'm so very sorry." Harry then picked up his top hat and walked briskly down the aisle and straight out of the church. Sable and

Maria followed him. They found him in the car park, climbing as quickly as he could into his car. Sable knocked on his window. Harry lowered it but only to say, "I'm so sorry."

Sable was so angry. "You are a complete bastard!"

The car was moving and Maria pulled Sable out of the way. They watched Harry drive out and into the road.

"What a bastard!" shouted Sable.

As Harry drove away, all he could think of were Han Wei and Sofia.

Maria gave her friend a hug of affection and told her what to do next. They went back inside the church.

Standing in front of the congregation, it was up to Henry to take charge. He quietened everyone and called for calm.

"Ladies and gentlemen, my daughter is not going to marry this, now departed, rogue, so I suggest we all wait here for a few minutes while Gloria and I go next door and talk to the caterers. We'll be straight back."

While Henry and Gloria walked over to the church hall, Sable and Maria sat down in the vacant seats. Mr and Mrs Jones, parents of the disgraced groom, looked totally unsure what to do. Nobody had much sympathy for them and were pleased to see them depart.

Everyone was chatting and wondering. One couple agreed emphatically that Sable had done the correct thing; abandoning the wedding was far better than the prospect of a future divorce.

Henry and Gloria were relieved that the caterers were both friendly and so very accommodating. Flexibility was the key to good business. The boss said they could bring things forward – no problem, sir. Henry suspected that they might have had experience of this before. So Henry and Gloria returned to the church to inform the guests to wait just another ten minutes, and then they could all go through for some tea and sandwiches. The wedding cake was going to be repacked and put back into Henry's car.

21

"Postponed, did you say?"

"Yes, sir. Postponed."

Harry was in the office of his line manager, having telephoned him just before going to the office. Charles Murgatroyd was somewhat baffled, not finding it easy to get his mind round something quite like this. It was most irregular to postpone a wedding, surely?

Charles had another question. "So, let me get this right, you have not married due to–what–complications?"

As was the custom, or so he thought, Harry stood to attention whilst trying to make things clearer for his boss.

"That's right, sir. Parents agreed it would be sensible to postpone things; one could call it a delay, practicality, that sort of thing," said Harry, knowing full well that it was anything but. He just hoped things would not filter to this end of the building from Sable's end. But then Charles Murgatroyd was not the sort of person to listen to gossip, let alone believe it.

"So when will it take place, Harold?"

"Not sure, sir. Months, probably… I'd like to get back to work, sir, if I may."

"Yes, yes, of course."

Harry returned to his departmental duties, glad to be back at his desk. 'Relieved' might have been a better word.

**

Over the weekend, especially on the Sunday, Henry, Gloria, Sable and Maria got round the table to sort things out and find out if any loose ends needed to be tied up. All wedding presents had been returned, except a few that had arrived by post.

Sable wondered if Harry had remembered to cancel the hotel – as far as she was concerned, that was his responsibility. There was also the issue of the flat. Sable was welcome to use it, of course, but then so would Harry have been, if they had got married. Henry and Gloria thought it best if Sable gave notice on it. Maria agreed. They had to bury the painful past.

Gloria advised that Sable's wedding dress, as well as Maria's, should be put away in mothballs in a wardrobe. As far as they could tell, those were the most urgent jobs to be done. Gloria would write a letter to the vicar and thank him for handling such an unusual event so well.

Henry and Gloria couldn't thank Maria enough for saving Sable from what would have been a disastrous marriage. They all agreed that Harry was a bit of a bounder – he was clearly good at his professional life but found difficulty with his private life.

Maria was still keen to discover more about the 'Chinese tart'. Perhaps she would do some investigative work. They were all agreed that Sable would telephone her boss and explain, that due to certain complications, i.e. the groom's health, the wedding had been postponed. She would return to work immediately.

About two weeks later, Sable received an invitation to a drinks gathering to celebrate someone's promotion. The venue was the Royal Exchange in the City. She boldly asked if she could be permitted to take a girlfriend and was surprised to be allowed to. Sable thought it would be a way of thanking Maria.

There had been plenty of work for Sable and it took her mind off the past. On the day of the party she phoned Maria to give her instructions. She told her to take the Underground to Bank and then walk up the steps into the grand old Royal Exchange. They would meet inside the glass doors.

The Royal Exchange is situated between Threadneedle Street and Cornhill. As she had approached the building, Sable agreed that the Palladian columns at the west entrance were a sight to behold, as was the huge and spacious hall inside.

Sable was wearing a tight dark dress and she had also put on some jewellery. When Maria arrived, Sable fully approved of her dark blue dress. Both girls wore attractive high heel shoes.

They moved forward and were met by a young girl, carrying papers, who just wanted to know their names. She ticked them off and pointed them to the group, which was the party in question.

Sable had visited the building only once before and then only briefly. But, to Maria, this edifice in the heart of the City was a gem. The high ceiling and roof was just a wonder to behold. Sable had read the potted history by the entrance.

"Founded by the merchant, Thomas Gresham, in the sixteenth century," she informed Maria, before proudly continuing, "but after a succession of fires over the centuries, this present building was rebuilt in 1844 and opened by a young Queen Victoria."

"Sable, thank you," said Maria and smiled gingerly at her.

They joined the party and were soon given flutes of something sparkling to drink. "It's either champagne or the other," said Sable.

Maria had a sip. "Darling, don't be silly, it's champers."

Several girls then came up to them, introduced themselves and ushered them into the main body of the party. There were lots of young men present.

"Who's party is it?" Maria whispered.

"We'll find out shortly," said Sable as she scanned the faces.

Sable was surprised to have been invited to the event. Someone in her section in the Foreign Office had obviously put her name on the list, so the people surrounding her were a mixture of staff and guests. She then saw a familiar face but could not remember his name. "It would have helped if everyone wore their name badge," she told Maria, who entirely agreed with her. She then turned and almost knocked the glass out of his hand. "I'm so sorry." Sable was full of regrets.

The man looked at his jacket and there was no damage. "That's no problem. It's so easily done. By the way, I'm Michael Grantham. How do you do? Please call me Mike." He had a nice smile.

"Sable Fairfax. I'm in the Foreign Office. French and German."

As they were getting into conversation, Maria was able to observe them from her position not far away. She was in a small group, with the main subject of conversation focused on international relations. Maria was more than happy to listen to these Foreign Office staff, soaking up current affairs and making the occasional comment. But from her vantage point she was able to observe both Michael Grantham and Sable. He had what she would describe as a cheeky smile which made her wonder how genuine he was. And after her recent experience, she did not want Sable to make another mistake. She wondered if he was also a guest. Sable was in the process of discovering.

"I'm a property developer. Two of us – my partner – we have various houses in progress at present, some in E1 and E14 and also in the west, in Belgravia," said Mike.

He was then joined by a girl, who sidled in and put her arm round Mike and did the talking, "Has he told you? He's converting something for Hugh Mannston in Belgravia." The girl then looked at Sable. "I'm Beryl, by the way. Mike's my guest."

"Sable Fairfax."

Sable was then thinking fast. "So you're doing something for the new prime minister?"

"That's right, " said Mike. "It's his bolt hole, away from politics – or will be in due course."

"Belgravia, eh," said Sable, somewhat impressed. "Wow. How well do you know Belgravia, Mike?"

Mike looked at her with a cheeky smile. "Reasonably well. I live there."

Beryl then added her pennyworth. "It's a little place in Eaton Place, isn't it, darling?"

They were then interrupted by another waitress, bearing vol-au-vents. They all dived in. Sable took two – lunch seemed a long time ago. Suddenly their glasses were refilled with champers as they were called to be quiet. It was time for a short speech. As Sable listened to the speech she looked around for Maria. She saw her with a small group. She also wondered where Beryl worked. Foreign Office or was she from the Home Office?

Sable was keen to know what the prime minister had bought for his London retreat. How much did he earn? From whom had he borrowed?

Maria felt it was her duty to try to protect her friend, so she was keeping a close watch on her. She wondered who Sable had been talking to.

Later, they were all asked to toast the lucky gentleman on his promotion – he was shortly going overseas. Everyone clapped and applauded. Sable gradually edged her way towards Mike Grantham because she wanted to know more about him and his business. When he saw her, he welcomed her.

"Yes, it can be a risky business; you have to work out the arithmetic carefully and be able to borrow at the same time. Luckily, I have a good source of finance, as has my client, Hugh. But the purchaser has an added obstacle to climb – it's the dreaded stamp duty. We are hoping that the tall man in number eleven will finally come to realise that the rate is far too high and is stifling the housing market. We just hope he makes an announcement soon. It's a bit like death duties, a dreaded sort of tax."

Sable looked at him. "If it was set much lower, I suppose there would be far more transactions? Not just here but all over the country?"

Mike drained his glass. "Not bad stuff. Er, that is very true. Housing is a constant annual problem in this country. And at the lower end of the scale, where are we going to put all new immigrants?"

Sable shrugged her shoulders a little. "Initially, that's a headache for the politicians. I'm a Civil Servant – on the road to being a young diplomat."

Mike looked at her carefully. "Very good. Look, may I ask you for your email address? I've got a dinner coming up soon, in the City, and I may be allowed a guest, a female guest."

Sable reached in her small handbag and produced a business card. Mike took it with thanks. He said he would be in touch.

Maria had been observing some of the guests and what they were wearing. She was sure that one girl, with a very tight dress, was not wearing any panties. There was just no outline, anywhere.

Sable and Maria spent some more time circulating, talking to one or two government staff and a few other guests. Sable then pointed to the expensive little shops that occupied the perimeter. There were jewellers, watches, handbags, smart clothes, all for sale to anybody who wanted to shed a few hundred or thousand pounds from their bank account. Maria was impressed with the quality but shuddered at the prices. "My goodness, who can afford this?"

"How about bankers and businessmen?" ventured Sable. "Or rich and influential tourists."

Maria pointed. "And what's up there – those steps?"

The two girls disappeared up some corner steps and came upon a mural that depicted a significant event in

English history. They walked on and observed another and yet another, all depicting wonderful events in English history. Some were set in London while others were set elsewhere, such as Portsmouth where Lord Nelson departed from on his way to fight the Battle of Trafalgar south of Cadiz. Maria was mightily impressed. "This is fascinating, darling."

They looked at them all, soaking up some very modern English history. There were paintings of parts of London which were most impressive. Maria thought that every British schoolgirl should come here and include it in their curriculum.

By the time they had returned to the party, things were clearly coming to an end, with people drifting off. They tried to find the host and organiser but with little success.

Sable also scanned the horizon of heads to see if Mike Grantham was visible but with little success. So they departed. Subconsciously, she forgot all about him; she wondered if he was a predator. Was this the legacy of Harold Jones?

As they walked back to Bank station they concluded that it had been time well spent even if she would never meet that member of staff again.

Maria thought it was a good place for a big party – loads of space. "If you work in the City, I'm sure it's ideal. It depends who's paying, perhaps," added Sable.

A thought then crossed her mind. She had not heard from Henri for some time, and his father had not come over – pity.

***

About a week later Sable received an email at work which surprised her. It had come from Mike Grantham, the property developer. He reminded her that they had met quite recently at a party at the Royal Exchange. He was inviting her to be his guest at a forthcoming dinner in the City.

Sable opened the attachment, read it and printed it off. It was a black tie dinner at one of the halls in the City. She read that the Brewers were located in Aldermanbury Square. Well, why not, she thought. She should have a chance to talk to him and find out what he was really like, especially if they sat beside each other. She would try to look at the website on the day of the dinner.

Her parents were very pleased that she was going to go to the City. Her father had had some exposure to dinners in City livery companies – they were magnificent events, full of tradition, often with superb formal entertainment with classical opera singers.

"Make sure you don't drink too much, darling," her father cautioned her, with a smile. "Not too much port; it's very tempting."

Sable was working well in her job. She discovered she was learning much commercial French, something that was largely outside the scope of her straight university course, where she had had to concentrate on a lot of French literature, such as Gustave Flaubert, Victor Hugo and Voltaire. It was business French that she wanted and the Foreign Office was providing it. She would need these skills in her role as a diplomat overseas.

On the day of the dinner, she took a light suitcase, containing her black dress and her smart black highheels and tiny black handbag, to work with her. She was determined to have a reasonable day and just hoped no crises would develop. Timing would be important because he said his car would be outside her entrance at five thirty.

Sable managed to vacate her desk and reach the ladies room to change on time. She would change her shoes once they were in the City. As she departed the Foreign Office, she hastily made her way down to the street; she wondered how she would recognise the car. And then she saw Mike with the car door open for her. He was smiling grandly at her as she climbed in.

As Mike drove off into the London traffic, she was able to appreciate the surroundings. He was dressed in black tie and all ready for the event. But what was the car?

"This? It's called a hybrid: half electric and half petrol – Toyota. Damn clever, really. Electric for the cities and petrol for the open road. All cars will be like this one day, I hope." He gave her a big smile. "What do you drive, Sable?"

"I don't, at the moment."

"Mm, never mind."

They were on the Embankment. They would then head north into the City and find their way to Aldermanbury Square. As they stopped at some lights, he had a chance to admire her dress and her shapely legs. He liked what he saw.

"How was your day, Mike? Have you been out and about?"

As he eased the car gently forward he told her that his day had been spent at his desk in Belgravia. He couldn't risk being at one of his sites – that was a recipe for being late. "Look at those new buildings. Glass everywhere. Do you like them?"

She looked around her. "Sometimes. It depends what's inside. But it can give an air of transparency to your business, perhaps. Mind you, I wouldn't swap my lovely Foreign Office building for one of those. And if you walk down Millbank there are lots of old buildings housing government departments and many of them have been modernised inside, especially with new lighting."

They were almost there. He drove around looking for a parking space and soon found one. After paying the required amount of money, he went to open the door for her.

"I've just got to change my shoes when we get in."

As he escorted her, he filled her in. "We'll be announced at the reception, shake hands with the Master and Wardens and then move in and mingle with the great and the good. We'll each have a programme as well – the seating plan will reveal all the guests."

Sable's mind went back to the Dutch embassy. She asked Mike if there would be any politicians present, British or foreign.

"Sometimes, but generally this is not their territory; put another way, the City seldom invites them." They joined others and climbed the staircase with its lovely thick red pile carpet.

During the reception, Mike looked after her well, limiting himself to two glasses of champagne. They met people from industry, university researchers, a handful of brewers from southern England and some delightful ladies, all terribly well dressed. But as they moved carefully through the huge room, Mike's eyes were actually everywhere, settling on ladies, admiring their form as discreetly as he could. Sable discovered that one charming lady was a professor who was just about to take up her new post at Exeter University.

"They've offered me a job that I just could not refuse, and they help me with housing," she said. "But it does mean leaving the London area – and all this." She pointed at the wonderful room, the portraits, the glass chandeliers, the grand French clocks.

Sable smiled at her. "I'm training on the diplomatic side – Foreign Office – and this is my first time here."

"Well, enjoy it, my dear."

Not only was Mike gracing his eyes on the ladies – boobs, bottoms and all, but he also smiled warmly at one of the waitresses. She was quite small, had black hair cut in a bob and wore soft pink lipstick. Like all the staff, she was foreign. She wore a tight black skirt.

Very soon the beadle announced, with his gavel, that dinner was served. Mike took Sable's arm and gently escorted her into the queue. He glanced down and felt like appreciating the curvature of her bottom. He quickly checked himself and decided he would do it later, perhaps in the car. It was obvious to other people how much he clearly liked the lady on his arm – was he already in love with her?

Mike and Sable sat beside each other and were able to chat without too much difficulty; the noise level was such that conversations across the table were limited.

There were some dignitaries on high table. Sable consulted her programme and noted that one was a permanent under-secretary at the Department of Trade; the other guest beside the Master was a senior officer in the Royal Air Force.

After the hot cured salmon with basil risotto, which had been washed down with dry Jurançon 2011, they moved on to breast of Gressingham duck garnished with saffron potatoes and pickled red cabbage.

"What do you think of this menu, Sable?"

She turned to him. "It's new and unusual. I must take a copy back to mother. But duck is not really my choice. I would favour beef."

As the little waitress hovered beside Mike, he was greatly tempted to pinch her stern, as it was only inches from his arm. Again, he held back. He then recalled an instance on an airline flight where his neighbour had done something far worse to a pretty stewardess as she stretched across to serve someone. Her skirt had ridden up her thigh and he just could not resist. Instead of a slap, she just gave him a severe look and moved away. The temptation to pour red wine over his shirt must have been enormous. Mike started to giggle.

"And does this meet with your expectations, Mike?" Sable asked, wondering what the joke was.

"Yes thanks. Pretty standard. Everything sticks to a pretty good format. The clerk sees to that – he runs the place."

Sable nodded. "And how often do you see Hugh Mannston?"

After drinking some more of the lovely wine, Mike recalled the last visit. "He comes round from time to time to view progress, complete with his security guard. He loves London and is looking forward to becoming a permanent resident – one day."

"Is he married?"

"No, I think he's a bachelor. Single, anyway."

Sable reminded herself to do a search on him next day.

The gentleman on her right then got into conversation with her. A kindly-looking man – he told her that he was a brewer from East Sussex. He had suffered in the river floods of 2000 when half his house was underwater. At first he and his family had relocated to a hotel which was up in the town on high ground. When the full extent of the damage was known, they rented a house for many months. The smell of decay inside his house had been simply terrible due to river water. Fortunately, the floods had not returned and his business was still good.

The meal had progressed. Mike turned and, with a cheeky grin, told her that he liked a good tart. At first Sable was shocked before realising that he was referring to the mango and chocolate tart which formed their dessert. Then she wondered if he had ever been with a tart in London. She thought it quite possible. It would have been an experience for him.

She then found her port glass was filled with ten-year-old tawny port. And she remembered what her father had said – go easy. The taste was magnificent, just like velvet.

This was then followed by a toast to the Royal Family. Luckily, she still had some wine remaining.

Guests were then offered a choice of either coffee or tea. To her intense surprise, the tea had been grown in Cornwall. She would definitely show this to her parents. Was this a result of climate change? Could it compete with Indian tea?

As she sat through two speeches, one of which was a response, she admired the collection of paintings.

After they had retired, there was a final chance of a short drink in another room. This allowed the guests to make a few more acquaintances before they had to depart. Mike put his arm around her and gave her a hug, which she liked.

During the course of the dinner they had encountered a brewer, a judge, and two senior servicemen. Not a bad night's work, she thought.

Once in the car, Mike offered to drive her all the way to her front door. "Darling, I am happy to do it."

It was the first time he had called her 'darling'. He took her hand and gave it a kiss.

"Mike, that's terribly sweet of you but I do live with my parents. I can't just invite you in. I hope you understand that. I'll be just as happy if you drop me at Waterloo and I'll catch a late train. Believe me, I've done it many times before… Another time."

He accepted that and drove her to Waterloo station. She did not want to tell him about the flat that she and Harry had planned to live in for a short time. It was temporarily sublet. What she wanted was a house.

As he dropped her he called out, "You must come to Belgravia some time. But thank you for coming tonight, Sable – so glad you enjoyed it."

"I'd love to. See you soon, Mike."

She hoped that was a positive enough statement. Then she turned and walked into the long concourse.

She looked at the board and saw a train for soon after eleven. That would suit her well.

There was one more working day ahead, the dinner having been held on the Thursday night.

She waited until her lunch break before searching for biographical details on Hugh Mannston. He appeared to have had a quiet enough early life in south-east England. He had attended Eton College and had then gone on to Oxford University where he read PPE. She searched around for other things, even looking for possible county court judgements against him, but there were none. There was precious little in the scandal department and no evidence that he might be the father of some illegitimate children. The slate was pretty clean and still unmarried. Noble chap, she thought. But then she discovered that he was a friend of a Russian oligarch who owned a big house, also in Belgravia. This particular Russian owned a huge yacht, usually seen in the blue waters off the South of France. Sable wondered if he was the source of Hugh Mannston's borrowed cash.

About a week later, and after several phone calls, Sable was on her way to have dinner at Mike's house in Belgravia. It was a Friday night. Another couple would be there, in the form of Tom and Suzie. And Sable had warned her parents that she might be home either very late or not until the Saturday.

Equipped with the address, Sable made her way there by public transport. The evenings were getting lighter, so she knew she would have a chance to take in some of the exterior of Mike's modest pile of bricks, as he euphemistically called it.

It turned out to be much larger than she thought. She actually thought he had been joking about it, but no, this was a good-sized Belgravia townhouse. She was impressed.

Tom and Suzie knew the house already so, leaving them in the courtyard garden, Mike took Sable round his modest 'little estate,' as he called it. He showed her the kitchen-diner and hallway, all of which were white. Then there was the small swimming pool which had an entrance leading off to the underground car park. Sable just loved it.

"Do you swim?" he asked.

"I can, but seldom get the chance – or the time."

Then they moved up the elegant staircase to view four bedrooms, all with fitted wardrobes complete with mirrors. In addition, there were four bathrooms complete with shower attachments. On each of the landings there was a collection of prints from English literature. She just loved viewing The Lady of Shalott and then round the corner she found Ophelia. There were also some light windows in the ceiling which brought in the light on a dark winter day.

"Naturally it has been modernised but essentially it is 1830s – sort of the Regency period."

Sable just loved it. "Mike, it has grandeur and elegance. It is just wonderful. Clever you."

Back downstairs, Tom was undoing the champagne which he had supplied for the dinner.

"We've actually brought two bottles, in the fridge, Mike," said Suzie with a wide smile.

Mike looked at his watch. "That chappie should be here in about twenty minutes." He turned to Sable. "I'm having dinner delivered."

"I'll be happy to help," said Sable very willingly.

While the two men were busy with glasses and the first bottle, Suzie took Sable aside and asked her what she thought of the house. She was certain it was between four and six million pounds.

Sable knew you could easily buy houses here for twice that sum at least. "Well, I think it's quite big enough for one person but it's surely a family home?"

Suzie agreed. "Oh yes, but he needs a good wife. Tell me, are you single or married?"

Sable was surprised at the question. She thought it would have been obvious. Without going into too much detail about a certain Mr Jones, prime bastard, she told Suzie very truthfully that she had been concentrating on her career. "Foreign Office – French and German."

Suzie was mightily impressed. "I still struggle with English, darling."

Sable had some news. "I haven't told Mike yet, but I'm going to France shortly for a one month assignment. There's a consulate that needs some help and it will be jolly good commercial experience for me."

"Sounds wonderful," said Suzie as she caught Tom's eye, who beckoned them over for drinks.

After toasting their host, Mike had to run to the kitchen with dinner that had just arrived. Tom went to give him a hand, leaving the girls to enjoy the champagne.

"Mm, I once had an uncle who regularly drank it with his breakfast," giggled Suzie. "Would you believe it?"

"Well it does rather lend itself to any time of the day, don't you think?" added Sable. They were then summoned.

The meal was Chinese and was piping hot. They were told to help themselves as dishes were handed round. Sable dived in and simply loved the King prawns. She also ate an abundance of cashew nuts, which startled Suzie.

The second bottle of champagne was most welcome and kept everybody in high spirits. When asked about his neighbours, he said he knew people on one side but not on the other. Tom told him to search through the internet – there were bound to be Arabs and Russians.

When the evening came to a close, Tom and Suzie said their farewells and wished Sable a successful career.

Once all the plates were in the dishwasher, Mike knew he had to take Sable home. He came up to her and put his arms round her. "Darling, you were wonderful. Did you enjoy it?"

It was so obvious that she had. She gave him a kiss whilst savouring his strong aftershave fragrance. She indicated that it was rather late to be going home. Then, in a particularly gallant gesture, he picked her up and carried her upstairs. They entered his bedroom whereupon he put her down.

He pointed. "If you use that bathroom, darling, I'll use another."

"You have a choice, darling, I counted four," she said as she disappeared.

Fortunately, she was still on the pill so she was able to enjoy her lovemaking without worrying. Mike was strong yet gentle and she felt comfortable in the various positions that they used.

When morning broke, she was surprised that it was eight o'clock. It must have been the champagne. At least she felt rested.

During breakfast he offered to drive her to her home and he wondered if that would be acceptable. Sable said she would phone her mother soon and see what they planned for the day – it was a Saturday after all.

"Lovely coffee, darling. Thank you." Sable was on her third cup.

Mike's phone then rang. He looked at it and realised who it was. He picked it up and walked to his office, telling Sable to carry on.

Alone in the kitchen, Sable phoned Gloria. Her mother was pleased that all was well and that she had enjoyed the dinner party. Sable said she would be home in the morning. Her father might do some shopping but otherwise Gloria would be there. Sable hinted that Mike could be bringing her.

"I'll be here, darling." Gloria hung up.

When Mike emerged he said that he had just been talking to his client, Hugh, who wanted to view progress on his 'bolt hole', as he always put it. Mike could see Sable was thinking, so he explained, "That was the PM. He's going to Chequers on Sunday, so he wants to see it today. We discussed things, so he's coming to see me early tomorrow on his way to Chequers. I hinted that this afternoon might be a bit tight. The PM seemed happy enough. Eight tomorrow it is."

"I'd like to meet him one day, Mike."

"Oh, I'm sure you will. Nice chap. Loves his London."

With Sable directing him, Mike drove through the Saturday traffic and headed down towards Clapham and the A3. After bypassing Putney and Kingston Upon Thames, they were soon close to their destination.

At the front door, Sable reminded Mike of the surname. When Gloria opened up, she was pleased to see her daughter in one piece and smiling happily. Sable quickly introduced Mike.

"Very pleased to meet you, Mrs Fairfax." Mike gave her a genuinely warm smile. Gloria looked at them keenly before inviting Mike to come in. She still carried a number of painful memories of Harold Jones.

"Henry's just come back from the shops."

"Plenty of bread, Stilton and, oh yes, celery," came a voice from the kitchen. Henry then emerged and kissed his daughter before shaking Mike's hand. Henry ushered them. "Come along in. Let's have a quick drink before a late lunch. Is that all right, darling?" Henry consulted Gloria, who agreed.

Henry opened a bottle of sparking Italian wine, which everyone would enjoy. He soon got into conversation with Mike and was naturally surprised that Hugh Mannston was one of his clients.

"Mm, tell me more, what's he like?"

"He's actually very nice, very focused on his job and seldom divulges anything – you know, keeps things close to his chest," said Mike.

"Much of what he does must be highly confidential?"

Mike agreed, "Oh yes. But he's got this thing about wanting to retire to Belgravia one day, hence this project of his. It's smallish but I'm converting a sort of studio."

Henry gave his approval. "If he likes London, why not. There's nothing like investing in property."

Mike continued, "I once went to a reception at Number 10 and was surprised how spacious it actually is. It goes back a long way. But the flat could be bigger."

The girls were partly listening to Mike, and Sable was longing to see this little studio, as he called it. Gloria then disappeared to prepare lunch.

It was over lunch, as they were talking, that Gloria did her best to keep her beady eye on Mike, just to see if there were any obvious cracks. If there were, she would point them out, firstly to Henry and then to Sable. She did not want another Harold Jones; he had really blotted his copy book. Mind you, as she recalled it, her daughter had really gone to town – quite unthinkable to make a fierce speech like that in church and show up his weakness in front of everybody! Had he really deserved such harsh treatment? Sable said yes. The man was clearly a bastard.

She wanted her daughter to marry a gentleman, preferably English. Surely that was not too much to ask?

Mike expanded a little on his business. He and his partner were into new builds and sometimes add-ons. They had found quite a lot of work prospects in the East London postcodes, both north and south of the river.

"And your parents, Mike, are they nearby?" Gloria wanted to know.

"In Hampshire, not too far away," said Mike.

They had a happy lunch. The soup was Gloria's best, while Mike devoured a plentiful quantity of Stilton and celery. "Jolly fine stuff," declared Mike.

"Do you do your own cooking, Mike?" asked Henry, knowing what the answer would be.

"Yes, but I have a cleaner once a week." She was a good little scrubber but he kept those comments to himself.

They had coffee in Henry's new conservatory. Sable explained that Mike had an early start on Sunday as he was expecting the PM's car.

"Have to see Hugh tomorrow – got to show him the state his little bolt-hole is in before he goes to handle affairs of state at his Buckinghamshire bolt-hole."

"Does he have a girlfriend?" asked Sable.

Mike shrugged his shoulders. "No idea."

Aware she might be away soon, she thought she would wait until she knew the date – she would find out next week.

Mike looked at the time and knew he ought to go. He consulted Henry on the best route into south-west London and then to the Victoria area. Henry thought the route up through Putney and Chelsea might not be too busy at this hour. Gloria wondered if Chelsea had been playing. Mike nodded his head in thought.

Sable kissed Mike goodbye and waved at the car as it motored out of sight. She ran back in.

"What do you think?" asked Sable, eagerly.

"Well, he seems nice enough, darling. I hope he's a good businessman as well," commented her mother.

Henry was in thought. "Darling, find out the name of his company, would you? Let me know?"

"Right. Yes of course." Sable always did what her father recommended, especially when it came to business and investment.

Next morning, Mike phoned Sable to tell her that the meeting with Hugh – as he liked to call him – had gone well enough. They were almost at the stage when they were discussing colour of floor tiles, patio tiles, and other internal features. Mike added that Hugh had arrived with his secretary and one security guard. Another car was already on its way to Chequers with two Sunday guests.

It was on the following Tuesday that Sable was told of her fairly imminent departure to Lyon, where she would spend a month working with the staff of diplomats. She was really very pleased to be going. The Consular Office was keen to have her for a month. Two staff were currently sick, one with a troublesome pregnancy. If all went well, that member of staff would in due course be on maternity leave anyway. Sable's assignment could be extended if necessary.

That night, Sable phoned Mike to tell him. He was kind and supportive, but not unduly worried; it would give him time to play the field again. However, he had intense respect for her.

Sable sent an email to Henri, informing him of her plans. She said she liked the idea of being in such an attractive spot, south-west of Geneva and situated on the River Rhône. Was there any chance he could come down for a weekend? She would give him likely dates

– the second would be best? Alternatively, she would return to London via Paris at the end of her assignment.

Her parents were terribly pleased for their daughter to be going on a proper assignment, and to France, especially. They were thrilled for her. When Henry consulted the atlas, his eyes settled on north-eastern France. He located the town of Metz which was in Alsace and once part of Germany, from 1870 to 1918.

"Another time, darling, try to get to Metz. You could practice both your French and your German," said Henry.

Sable smiled. "I agree, Daddy, but we may not have a Consular Office there. I might have to go there purely as a tourist."

Henry looked disappointed. "Oh."

22

As Sable was packing her bags for France, she wondered how true and faithful Mike would be. He had given her every indication that she was a super girl and right for him and he had shown her his home in Belgravia. She had loved it. But was he going to behave himself in her absence? She might discover one day. As for herself, not engaged or committed, she was still a free agent.

She had asked personnel if they could send her down by train and they were very happy to oblige. Having said goodbye to her parents, she got herself to St. Pancras International where the Eurostar whisked her to Paris Gare du Nord. She then took a taxi to the Paris terminus for east and south France, the Gare de Lyon. In no time at all, the express TGV departed on time and was soon racing through the attractive French countryside which gave her a chance to appreciate the farming landscape.

Some of the French passengers must have been seasoned travellers because some of them pulled out well prepared picnic boxes. Sable was most impressed with their sense of practicality. Unable to compete with them, she went to the buffet car where she simply had coffee and sandwiches. She assumed she would be at a hotel that night in Lyon.

She then reflected on the men in her life. Mike was very nice, had a lovely house and knew how to entertain. But how loyal would he be? Then there was the Dutch prime minister, who knew a pretty girl when he saw one and was prepared to chase her if he had to. He was attractive, but a married man. And finally there was Henri, a slightly shy and cute young man, whom she hoped would swiftly mature. He appeared rather innocent and charming and he was not somebody you would intentionally want to hurt.

Of the three, Mike had the most stable job and a career ahead of him. The Dutchman was a politician, here today but could be gone tomorrow. While Henri was looking for something suitable in Paris.

Soon they were entering the long station in Lyon. Known as Gare de la Part-Dieu, it was the primary railway station in Lyon, with a good connection to Marseille. Sable stood and admired the overhead electric lines before pulling her suitcase towards the exit.

Once outside, she hailed a taxi and asked for the British Consular Office at 24 rue Childebert. Had she known the city well, she could have taken a tram.

***

Back in London, Mike was in a bar in Belgravia. He had had a long day and he felt he needed to relax. He was sitting at the bar and there were two pretty girls to his left, perched on bar stools. They both wore tight, black miniskirts. Mike wondered why they were there.

Suddenly Mike's phone gently rumbled. He viewed it and saw an email from Sable. Excited, he turned away to get more light and read the message. Sable was in her hotel room in Lyon, having eaten dinner and was preparing for a good sleep. She said the train journey down from Paris had been most impressive. The British consul had been most kind and had installed her in the modest hotel. She would start her first day tomorrow.

Mike wished her well and sent his love. He then went back and sat at the bar, ordered another beer and sat there eating peanuts and green olives.

The girls then turned to Mike and one of them spoke. "Our glasses are empty. You couldn't be a dear, could you?" She smiled at him.

Mike wondered if these girls were looking for business. He asked them what they wanted and then he asked the barman to do the honours. "Sorry to spoil your fun, girls, but I'm going home in a moment. Tomorrow is a working day for me." And probably a working night for them, he thought. Annoyed that Mike was going, the girls sat drinking and looking round the bar.

Once he was home, he checked his diary to see where he had to be on the following morning. He then went to bed.

Next morning, Sable used a street plan provided by the consul and walked to the consulate. She found rue Childebert quite easily. Once she had arrived he gave her his undivided attention.

William Tidyman was tall and thin and invited her to call him Bill. Everybody did. "I'm sure you will find this work quite easy, and probably less demanding than London but you will have a chance to meet the public in the visa section. People come in with all sorts of problems. You'll soon get used to the dialect; this is not quite the same as the language laboratory in university," he warned her with a smile.

"I'm sure I'll cope, Bill" she said.

"I'll be taking you out to lunch, it being your first day. Thereafter you can do as you please – café, sandwiches, etc. We have a kitchen area upstairs. In winter some of the girls bring in thermos flasks full of soup. Even my wife does it sometimes."

Sable worked at her desk all morning, reading correspondence. There was another box full of letters and applications, many of which had never been opened. She knew there was a staff shortage, but this was just not right. She would have to tackle it. She might even mention it over lunch.

By the end of her first week she had demonstrated her skills at mucking in. All the old correspondence had been opened and sorted, but not yet answered. She had got to grips with the local dialect but still found some of the somewhat less educated customers a bit of a handful.

She told them as politely as possible that sometimes things took a little bit longer, especially when a bureau was understaffed. One unhappy woman actually used the word 'merde' as she departed.

She learnt that Lyon was the first town to have a stock exchange, or bourse, and the first to issue cheque payments. She had heard of the bank Credit Lyonnais; she also discovered that Lyon was once a great silk manufacturing centre.

When asked if she liked walking, one of the girls suggested that she spend a weekend exploring the city centre right down to the end of the peninsular. With the Rivers Rhône on one side and the Saône on the other, the city centre was known as the Presqu'ile.

The consul reported back to London that Sable had done so very well in a short space of time and had reduced the mountain of paperwork to a manageable level. She was a very keen member of staff. This was duly noted on Sable's personnel progress file and they noted that Sable was doing the work of two people.

By now Sable was staying in what they called the company flat. This was ideal because her friend, Henri, was coming down from Paris to stay the next weekend. They could do their own catering. She decided she would show him old Lyon, as well as the Roman city area located on Fourviére Hill.

Henri was overjoyed to see her and to commemorate their meeting he had brought some red roses. Sable responded by giving him a hug and a passionate kiss. Their time in Paris was suddenly alive again but this time in another French city. Even when they were doing the washing-up in the little kitchen, the sexual chemistry was all too obvious. He couldn't keep his hands off her.

"Oh, my parents asked to be remembered to you," he said.

"And please give them mine. I have fond memories," she said as she led him into the rooms. "We only have single beds, Henri, as you can see. Not my planning, I assure you. So, if you are happy with that room, I'll stay here. How about breakfast at nine followed by sightseeing?"

Henri nodded and smiled in agreement. He kissed her goodnight and asked if he could use the bathroom first.

"This really is a step back in history," he said as he admired the Renaissance houses on the west bank of the River Saône. They were viewing Old Lyon. To reach it they had walked westwards across one of the bridges that led into Vieux Lyon. Most of the Renaissance houses were constructed around a courtyard, which was reached from the street through a vaulted passage beneath a house. As they were to discover, in each street a few courtyards had another vaulted passage at the back leading into the next street. They walked through one of the public passages, called traboules. They stood and looked. Sable recalled her time in Berlin and visiting some of the underground shelters.

"I bet these walls could tell stories – eh, Henri?"

"Quite fascinating," he said, as he took it all in.

"I wonder if Jews hid here during the Occupation? I bet they did. Some of the very old residents might know. My god, it must have been shocking."

Sensing her sadness, Henri gave her a hug.

"Just think of the deportations from here to Poland by cattle truck, right up until Liberation." Both of them tried to imagine how ghastly it would have been and how lucky they were to be alive in a Europe at peace.

"When was that?"

"Hang on," she said, "Third of September 1944, by the Americans and the French."

They then walked over to admire the Hotel de Gadagne, the finest Renaissance mansion in Lyon. They photographed it several times although she thought it was slightly disappointing. Sable would send a photo to her parents – her father would like it.

After lunch they visited the fourteenth-century cathedral of Saint Jean and they marvelled at the remarkable astronomical clock, still in working order.

"Damn clever," commented Henri.

Once outside, Sable recommended some exercise. "Fancy a climb – Fourviére Hill." And so they climbed up the steep hill, being overtaken by funicular cable cars. But it was well worth it. They found themselves facing what looked like a white limestone building, built in the rococo style. Complete with four towers, it had a terrace overlooking the city and the rivers to the east.

The view was amazing. This was Notre-Dame de Fourviére.

"I would call this a basilica – on a par with Sacré Coeur in Paris," said Henri.

Sable nodded her agreement. "True. What I would call Victorian. Hang on – yes, 1884," That is what her tablet read.

This was the first time that she had properly been with Henri. They were tourists and clearly enjoyed being together. London suddenly seemed a long way distant. Henri outlined his plans to try to qualify for the French Corps Diplomatique. Speaking fluent English was a bonus but he felt he ought to learn perhaps an Eastern European language, to make himself more marketable and to have an additional skill to offer.

"Yes, you don't want to work in a Consular Office all your life; it's a bit limited. Darling, you must aim for an ambassadorial appointment."

He turned to her. "But why are you here, Sable?"

She explained that it was a sort of cover post, while two staff were absent. It also gave her an insight into routine life in a Consular Office and the paperwork involved, plus the chance to learn a different French dialect. Meeting the French public across a glass window was also an experience.

"Now then, my darling, tomorrow we will visit these places that lie across the river over there." She pointed at her map. Arm in arm, they slowly walked back to the company flat. Before reaching it, Henri took her into a small brasserie to have a drink.

"This town is full of hidden gems," recalled Henri with a cheerful smile.

"Are you pleased you came, Henri?"

"Oh Lord yes, Sable." Henri took her hand and gave it a chivalrous kiss.

Sable wanted to fall in love with him but he was still somewhat immature. However, she regarded him as deeply trustworthy, and that counted for a lot. He was also a loyal and dependable friend.

After a decent night's sleep, they breakfasted at nine thirty. They planned to do some sightseeing before going to the station to catch Henri's train home.

The sun was out and the day was bright. Sable and Henri walked hand in hand, happy to be together. As they passed a Chinese restaurant, she wondered how her dear friend, May Ling, was getting on. They were soon on the peninsular and walking in a northerly direction.

She looked at him. "Do you like fine arts?"

"Oh yes. Always interesting," said Henri, positively.

"Well, I think there's quite a variety in the museum, so we might recognise some of the schools," she added. "We're pretty well served in London."

"But did you know the city was famous for silk-weaving – for generations. From thousands of small workshops they furnished the museums and palaces of Europe."

It took Sable by surprise. "Really?"

Well, he should know; this was his country, not hers. Being a Sunday, there was less traffic than on a weekday, but still plenty of pedestrians.

Soon they had reached the museum and made their way into the rooms. Luckily, they both enjoyed what they saw and were able to exchange sensible comments. This pleased Sable; she thought back to some of her earlier experiences, especially when she was a teenager, going round with friends who just did not even want to try to appreciate fine art. Such experiences were hard work and boring.

They had lunch at a brasserie nearby and were able to sit out. They both agreed that the Dutch paintings were vibrant. Looking at the clock, Sable and Henri moved on and it was only a short walk to the city hall, dated July 1886.

She pointed. "Now that to me is a wonderful 'Victorian' building. Just look at its architecture."

They both acknowledged that it was a sight to feast their eyes on – a marvellous piece of work. "Almost better than Paris," said Henri.

From there they swiftly walked back to the flat to collect Henri's luggage. Once ready, they took the tram to the train station.

"Please give my very best wishes to your parents... I'm so pleased you came. Get home carefully, darling."

She gave him a big hug and a kiss before the train departed.

As she walked past a newsagent, she saw a magazine carrying a picture of the Dutch prime minister with a lovely young lady on his arm. She read the headline. It was not his wife, but a new politician who had recently joined his party. He appeared to be giving her a squeeze all over her breasts, which were not exactly small. And she was just loving the publicity.

"I must teach him a lesson one fine day," she said out loud.

The vendor, who knew a little English, looked at her. "Mr Schmidt, do you know him, mademoiselle?"

Sable was caught offguard but managed a smile at the man. "The last time I saw him was in London," she chuckled. "I'm working here in the British Consulate for a few weeks. Good to meet you, monsieur."

They smiled at each other and she then took the tram back to the company flat. Once there, she sat down and felt very flat and deflated. She and Henri had got on so well and had enjoyed a wonderful weekend. She missed him immediately after he had gone.

What could she do, she wondered? She missed him more than she missed Mike. And was Mike even thinking of her?

She then sent a message to her mother, telling her that she had had a lovely time and defining some of the places that they had visited. She even suggested that her parents could choose Lyon for a short holiday one day, perhaps travelling by train. It was a lovely city – three days might be enough for them.

***

"Are you agreeable to go back to London in ten days' time?"

She was sitting opposite Bill, who struck her as being a very ordinary consul and not particularly ambitious. "Yes, of course. I should have cleared pretty well everything by then and hand over a clean slate."

Bill made a note in his large paper diary. She was glad to see that she was not the only member of the Foreign service to use traditional diaries. They were so much more reliable and far faster to make an entry. When she opened her diary, the whole week was on display – it was very sensible.

"Good. Well done, Sable. And have you managed to see something of the city?"

Sable told him about her friend who had managed to come down for just twenty-four hours in a cheap hotel. Bill just smiled and did not ask any questions. She told him how much they had loved the basilica on the hill.

"Ah yes, quite a building," was his comment.

She reminded him that she would be returning by train, via Paris. She then went to her office and got on with some routine work before doing a short stint on the front desk. She helped a young British couple and then did her best to give advice to some French youths wishing to work in London.

She then sent a friendly message to Mike, giving him an indication of when she would be returning and also a follow-up message to Henri. He replied immediately, saying how much he missed her.

In her remaining spare time she visited a few churches, museums and bistros. She also made a note to visit the well-known brasserie in Stratton Street, London just a few yards from Green Park Underground station. She wondered if it was supposed to be French.

23

Once back home, her father was so very pleased to see his daughter. She was clearly making good progress and he hoped that personnel were now more fully aware of her skills and capabilities.

Once back in the familiar settings of her office, which she had missed, she was soon summoned by her boss. It was a new boss; there had been a change in her absence. The words 'patron' and 'chef' were used commonly in France so Sable had to remind herself now to stick to Anglo-Saxon formalities instead, but only where appropriate. This would also apply to staff who were under her wing. She had hardly been aware of his existence, but her new boss was Mr Miles Copeland. He was of medium height and looked decent enough. She had seen his name somewhere but could not quite place it.

"Good to see you, Miss Fairfax. Sable, is it? Right." He looked over some papers and was satisfied that this was all in order. "Bill Tidyman, our consul in Lyon, was most impressed with all the work and organisation you did. So well done. I gather you also met the public. Anyway, we want you to oversee some of our staff here, new staff in places, and you will be interacting with several departments. As you know, most of our larger embassies have several departments." He paused to think for a moment. "Yes, one of my cousins is a Cultural Attaché somewhere. So, are you interested? - and with it comes promotion to second secretary."

Sable could hardly contain her surprise. She almost came out with a flurry of French words but checked herself just in time. "Please. When do I start?"

Miles Copeland smiled at her. "Well, can you start tomorrow? Finish what's on your plate today then get ready to supervise these staff. You can meet them all tomorrow. Now the real component of your job will start in about two weeks' time. You'll be assistant private secretary to the permanent under-secretary – that's Sir Giles Sloane. You'll meet him soon. There will be quite a lot of politics involved, so keep reading the newspapers, political and foreign news. Anyway, make a start on this first." He handed her some sheets of paper containing names and departments and range of languages spoken. "It's a bit of a rush but I am sure you can cope?"

She smiled at him and stood up.

"This recommendation comes from personnel/HR, so well done, Sable," he said.

"Thank you, Miles."

Back at her desk Sable sat down to do some thinking. She hoped this was all part of a plan to groom her for a longer-term posting, hopefully somewhere in Europe. After being a student in both Paris and Berlin, and this recent job in Lyon, she was keen to show her mettle in one of their European embassies. She then picked up the pile of dossiers and walked off briskly in search of a Mr Howard.

It was not quite two o'clock so he still thought he had enough time to play around. As Sable approached his chair from behind she could see he had an iPhone and an iPad, as well as his computer. Goodness, she thought, are they really governed by these gadgets? She stood by his desk and coughed politely. Rising to greet this unknown woman, Howard managed to drop everything on the floor.

She extended her arm. "Sable Fairfax, second secretary, your new boss, as they say."

"Yes, of course, John Howard. Pleased to meet you, Miss Fairfax."

She looked at him with some authority. "If you can drag yourself away from these games, please follow me." Other members of the section watched keenly as John Howard meekly followed Sable down a corridor and eventually along to her office. "Please, sit down, John." John sat in one of the upright chairs opposite her desk. "So, what's your speciality, John?"

He was unsure what she meant. Was she referring to his computer games? He thought for a moment. She then cut him off.

"Well, is it defence studies, current affairs, commerce and trade? Or are you learning Cantonese and Mandarin at night school?"

He stumbled a bit. "Well, neither, Miss Fairfax. It's largely Central European languages and the politics that goes with it. I like to think I help with trade between our country and theirs."

"Very good, John." She scanned down his file to look at recent experience and to see if he had been anywhere. She looked up at him and thought she was looking into the eyes of a scared rabbit caught in the headlights. She smiled at him. "John, I'm just trying to get to know you and learn about your strengths. That's rather important. Tell me, do you have many friends in the Foreign Service?"

He began to open up. "My friend, Richard, has been in Japan for almost a year now. He tells me that he's thinking of getting married to a Japanese girl. He recently sent me a photo of the two of them, somewhere in Tokyo."

Sable nodded. "Very commendable. And what do you think he ought to do?"

"Well, that's a tough question, Miss Fairfax. If he loves her, then they ought to get married."

Sable thought for a moment. "It's a very different culture out there. I wonder if she has ever been to London? He really needs to introduce her to the English countryside so that she can appreciate English or Anglo-Saxon culture. Cities are rather different. They are big, noisy, and with international populations, and they seldom sleep. Have you ever walked along Oxford Street at a weekend?"

"I don't go shopping much," he said mildly, as he shook his head a little.

"You are hard-pushed to find a truly white English person amongst the crowd. It's so very cosmopolitan." She looked at him.

"But surely good for business? Loads of tourists – Arabs and the like?"

"I totally agree with you. Hopefully they all have money to spend. Now Tokyo is a very big international city, like London and Hong Kong." She then went on to discuss the merits of marrying a city girl or a girl from the country who has had to get used to city life. And did his friend like Japanese culture? Was he prepared to adapt to it and get used to very different in-laws?

The young man opposite her told her what he knew of Japanese foreign policy and their defence industry. The topic of energy and the electronics industry also cropped up. Soon they were talking about China and electric cars of the future.

It was time to close up the conversation. "Right, John. You know my door is always open." She stood up. "Good to have met you. Please, carry on."

Politely dismissed, he walked back to his desk, but glad to have met his new boss.

Meanwhile, Sable was looking at the next names on the list. She also made a note to do a search of German car manufacturers likely to produce more hybrid cars: she was sure that was where the future lay. She then spent the rest of the afternoon familiarising herself with two more members of her team. She wanted to adopt a style that would make her a liked person and be known as an approachable person. But she needed to be authoritative as well, when the situation demanded it.

Back home at the end of the day, she had a chat with her father about Japan. His mind quite naturally went back to the days of the war in the Far East. He told Sable that Japanese soldiers regarded their emperor as a god, which was one reason why surrender in those days was unthinkable. But their economic recovery after 1945 had been truly remarkable. They had built up a superb electronics industry.

***

It was a Saturday afternoon and Mike had told her to meet him at the entrance to the tallest building in London. Sable had taken the train to London Bridge station and had then walked the short distance to the Shard.

He gave his girl a hug and a kiss and took her in towards the entrance. He pointed at the staircase.

"One can climb, or so I gather, but not today," he said as he watched the indicator board. Actually, they did not have too long to wait with the other tourists. Soon they were whisked upwards at a rapid speed. "Keep your mouth open, darling, we'll soon be at a height of two hundred and forty-four metres."

There was a general buzz of excitement amongst the tourists as they came closer to their destination. Sable was amazed when they exited on the seventy-second floor, the observation deck. In fact, they were all totally amazed when they found their feet and saw the view before them.

Mike put his arm round his girl in a protective way. And the buzz around them was palpable as the tourists began to take in the enormity of the view. The last time Mike had seen a really good view was from the observation gallery at the Tate Modern – it was from there that you had a really good view of the City from the South Bank of the Thames.

Mike ushered his girl and explained to her that, on a clear day, the view was a forty mile radius. Today it was quite good. "I hope you don't suffer from vertigo?" he asked.

She looked up at him. "I don't know, I mean, I won't know, will I, unless I get to the edge and have a panic attack?" Very sensibly she did not go quite up to the edge.

Mike looked around. "I think this is Western Europe's tallest building, in total a ninety-five storey skyscraper, would you believe?"

They carefully walked around, taking in the magnificent views in all directions. They both admitted it was unparalleled, a marvel of modern day engineering in concrete, steel and just masses of glass.

"Plenty of work for a window cleaner," she suggested.

"Come on, let's have some lunch."

Twenty minutes later they were devouring lobster salad with a sparkling white wine.

"Do you know, this building was designed by one Renzo Piano." Mike couldn't stop chuckling. "Amazing name."

"Well, he obviously hit the right note then!" she commented.

Mike then talked about his workload in east London, which was going well enough.

"And the bolt-hole for the PM?" she asked.

He nodded. "Yes. Slowly, slowly." He purposefully omitted to tell her that there was a slight labour dispute going on with the builders. But he was confident it would

soon be sorted out. He blamed the Poles.

Later, Mike was mesmerized when Sable devoured the cheese, biscuits and celery which the waiter had just delivered to their table. The stilton was gone in no time. So Mike hastily ordered some more. Poor girl, she must be really hungry. But he smiled.

He then put his hand in his pocket and placed a small black box on the table in front of her. "Darling, I have a little something for you. But firstly, here's to your health." He raised his glass and they toasted each other. "And now, my darling, if you open that, you will understand why you are here."

Sable was intrigued. She opened up the clasp and gasped as she saw inside. "The most important thing is to see if it fits, " was Mike's only sensible comment. Slowly, she removed the lovely ring and inserted it onto her engagement finger. The diamond appeared to be surrounded by small garnets. "Darling, are you happy to wear it?" Without waiting, he leant forward to give her a kiss.

"But, of course, Mike. It's just wonderful, darling."

"Well, are you happy to be engaged?"

She smiled happily. "Yes, thank you darling. So exciting." This unexpected news had done wonders for her appetite so she devoured some more cheddar, much to Mike's amusement. And instead of coffee, they drank a bottle of cool sparkling water.

The view from the restaurant was out of this world. Mike hoped it was a wonderful way for a couple to become engaged – it was certainly different.

After gazing at some of the sights and identifying a few landmarks, Mike excused himself to go to the WC. While he was gone, Sable crept up to the glass and rubbed the diamond apex against it. It made a furrow. She was satisfied this was diamond and not a cheap cubic zirconia, sometimes advertised in magazines and cheap newspapers.

"At least it's not crap," she said softly to herself before Mike had returned. But one thing he had failed to tell her was that, as a teenager once, he had been convicted for shoplifting. When they were ready, they took the lift to the ground. Once outside, Mike looked up. He told her it was one thousand feet to the very top.

"It is amazing," she admitted.

"Goodness knows what it must have cost – simply millions," he said. "I suppose that's one way to invest."

She looked at her watch, "Darling, have we time to go to my parents? And break the good news?"

Mike thought for a moment. "Yes. I don't have my car with me but I can always go home by train."

***

"Goodbye, Mike." They waved heartily.

"I'll take Mike to the station. Come on, darling," said Sable with enthusiasm, as she took his arm.

Henry and Gloria went inside to discuss, after hearing the good news and after meeting Sable's fiancé.

"Will they live there – I mean, in his Belgravia house?" asked Henry.

Gloria was surprised. "Of course, darling, where else?"

Henry had hoped they might have expressed a wish to buy a fresh matrimonial home, something virginal, even if it was in Belgravia.

"Silly not to use it when it's there, darling," chirped Gloria. "Stop being old-fashioned."

Henry nodded and then poured them both another drink. He sat in his chair and at that moment Gloria came and sat in his lap. She hugged him and kissed him.

"Darling, I am sure it will be fine. By all accounts it's a lovely house set in a magnificent position. Better than the flat that she and Harry were first going to live in."

"Quite," said Henry and again he nodded.

"The ring looks lovely," commented Gloria.

"I'm sure we'll hear in due course from Sable about when they want it and where. What do you think, darling, Central London?"

This time Gloria nodded. "Mm, could be."

***

Sable and Mike continued pursuing their careers as the weeks unfolded. Sable had to admit to her best friend, Maria, that being proposed to on top of the Shard would take some beating.

"Not many people can do that, darling," said Maria as she excitedly told Sable how thrilled she was with the good news over the phone. "When's it going to be?"

Sable enthused, "Mike wants to get through most of the summer but still plan a summer wedding. But he's got quite a lot of work coming up – the dear old honeymoon might have to be a long weekend somewhere, you never know. When Mike's working hard like this, he says he needs to be there."

Actually, Sable did not really mind. Right now their plan was for her to get acquainted with the house in Belgravia and her best route to the Foreign Office, which she already knew.

Amongst other things he had to do that day, Mike planned to take his fiancée to The Derby. He bought everything on the computer, as he had the previous year; only this year he was taking someone special.

They drove to Epsom from Oxshott along small country roads. Entering Epsom from the west, Mike followed the yellow signs and was soon approaching The Downs. His fiancée was wearing a deep blue dress, complete with hat and high heels. Mike was in morning clothes and he had chosen a blue tie.

The crowds were enormous. Everybody who was anybody was, of course, there. Once they were in the stand they were able to soak up the atmosphere which was full of intense excitement. Their programme showed that there were many races before the actual Derby, which was in the late afternoon.

Using his binoculars, which he carried round his neck, Mike watched some of the horses as they approached the stand. But he also took the opportunity to focus on some of the ladies in the crowd – it was always good to appreciate form.

The place was packed out. Mike took Sable to a bar where he ordered champagne. They sat on bar stools and simply admired some of the ladies' outfits as they passed by. It was most entertaining. Up on the high-level screen they could watch the races as they unfolded, followed by a mixture of cheers and groans as the results came in.

Mike knew next to nothing about horses, except they could be a worthy investment. But it was so often the jockey who made the race, and some jockeys were very skilful and they knew their horses very well.

"Many of them are Irish," commented Sable as she watched the screen. Mike nodded, smiled and agreed with her.

He and Sable had largely come for the socialising and the atmosphere but they would be out on the stand for the main event which was coming up soon. Mike then saw someone out of the corner of his eye; he excused himself on the pretext of a visit to the gents. Giving Sable a kiss, he quietly disappeared. Meanwhile, Sable's eyes were glued to the screen and the commentary.

A few minutes later, Mike was behind one of the tents with his former girlfriend who was there on a girls' day out. He had his hand all over her bottom and he was pushing himself against her, rubbing up against her breasts. Always one for a bit of physical action, she was half enjoying it and half trying to modestly push Mike away.

"Darling, we are not together anymore. Remember?" she said as she freed herself and tried to straighten the lower half of her dress. She discovered that her panties were all at an angle.

They were in a corner just out of sight. Mike's heart was racing. "You look stunning, my darling," said Mike, "And how are you these days?"

Having put herself back together, she told Mike that she was okay but simply had to get back to her girls.

"All right. Point taken," said Mike in a dejected way.

No sooner had he restored his hat, than she had gone. Momentarily he stood there, trying to work out where that relationship had gone wrong all those months ago. When he returned to Sable he found her in deep conversation with someone who knew the sporting world quite well. She introduced Mike as her fiancé and they suddenly all started talking about investments and risk. They all had something to say on the subject.

Suddenly they turned to the screen and saw the start of the Derby, so they rushed outside and found some space on the stands. The commentary became so very lively and almost noisy at the end that it was difficult to know who had won. Their friend had more or less broken even.

"I think I'll stick to building," said Mike.

"That's a safe bet, darling, " replied Sable. "My parents should have been watching the race as well."

Mike and Sable then went in search of the afternoon tea tent. He just hoped they would not bump into his old flame.

As they devoured a few sandwiches they watched the comings and goings. Whatever one might say of it, Derby Day was a great occasion in both the social and sporting calendars. It was a good day for making some money.

Mike and Sable then discussed the merits of attending Henley and Wimbledon or just one of them. She wondered if her new boss, Miles Copeland, ever ventured out.

"And don't forget, darling, somewhere in all this we've got to fit in our marriage," Sable almost exclaimed.

Mike took her hand. "Yes, darling, I do know. Well, we could bring it forward?"

"Yes, well, suits me," she said.

After further discussions, and finishing their pot of tea, Sable indicated there was somewhere she wanted to go. The clerk on the information desk gave them clear enough instructions. So without more ado they took the escalator to the next floor. Seeing the signs, they approached the VIP lounge. She then asked Mike to stay in the shadows while she checked something out. Slightly bemused, he did as he was told.

Sable then asked the doorman a few questions. In order to answer her, he had to check a computer list. Meanwhile, Sable had edged herself in a little and was able to search the horizon with her eagle eyes.

"No, madam, there's no record of the Dutch prime minister, I'm afraid. One or two ambassadors and their spouses, a few MPs and their spouses and as you can see, quite an entourage of owners from the Middle East. I can't help you further, madam. Sorry."

Sable was all smiles. "Oh don't worry further. You have been most helpful."

And with that she departed and swiftly put her arm inside Mike's and led him back down the escalator.

He looked at her, puzzled, "Everything all right?"

She just mumbled a 'yes'.

Having had the best of the day, they wandered back to the car. Amongst the topics on their agenda to discuss were when to get married and where. Mike suggested the Chelsea Register Office.

"I think my parents would favour our church. You don't mind, do you? They like tradition, Mike, so do I. But we would need to book it soon." She gave him a slightly penetrating look. "Shall I find out what's available?"

"Good idea," he said.

Mike drove Sable back home and was persuaded to stay for a light supper. They tried to explain that they had only recently had tea in the tent but Gloria was convinced they would have room for her Waldorf salad. Meanwhile, Henry and Mike drank some non-alcoholic beer which Henry had recently discovered in his supermarket. It was just the drink on a day like this, he said. "It's German. Well, not to worry," chuckled Henry.

During the course of conversation, Henry reminded people that wedding invitations were normally sent out four to six weeks before the date. Sable, of course, knew that only too well.

Sable looked at Mike. "Daddy, Maria was telling me the other day that a friend of hers had most of her

271

invitations sent out by email, with just four weeks' grace."

Henry was aghast. "My goodness, what has the world come to?"

Gloria smiled at her husband. "Darling, everything's digital these days."

"Terrible," muttered Henry, much to the amusement of everybody.

***

Back at her desk the next week, Sable received a message from Mike that he could obtain tickets for Wimbledon. How was she placed? Sable had to examine her diary very carefully. Having found a date, she then thought it only politic and sensible to ask Miles, her new boss. Having been given new responsibilities, she wanted to set a fine example. He was entirely happy with her course of action and wished her a happy day.

In return, Sable had been given some dates by Gloria, who had been in touch with the church. She put them to Mike.

***

There were people everywhere and they were nearly all dressed for the part. Amongst them was Sable who wore a cool summer dress while Mike wore a tropical suit. The day was hot but not too humid.

As they made their way to No. 1 Court, they passed a whole host of tennis enthusiasts and fans, all there for the action that afternoon.

Mike was sorry that he was not allowed to take his binoculars. He loved to admire people, whether it be players or spectators. He also liked to admire their clothing and see which brand they were sporting. And then there were the celebrities, usually to be seen occupying prominent positions. These were people from the world of film, television, the arts, sports celebrities and sometimes politicians. Prominent visitors from overseas could sometimes be seen.

They had come to watch a Ladies' Singles match, followed by a Mens' Doubles match. They agreed that if the Ladies' match turned into a marathon, they would try to extricate themselves and get a drink or afternoon tea. Even leaving a seat was governed by protocol, lest you disturb other spectators.

Sable was glad that the female players wore mostly white and observed the Club rules. Mike was glad that frilly panties were still occasionally worn.

"Is Hugh Mannston coming here this year?"

"I've no idea," said Mike. "He's probably far too busy in Parliament."

Later, over tea, they were caught devouring fresh strawberries by one of Mike's colleagues. He was keen to tell them that Wimbledon received a supply of freshly picked strawberries each morning – they were shipped in from the fields of Kent. After a ten minute chat he had to go and find his friends.

Sable suddenly turned serious. "Darling, three questions. Are you happy with that date? Have you bought the ring? Can you please book our brief honeymoon, as I gather you are in the midst of something?"

Mike was happy with the date and promised to phone the hotel as soon as possible in order to book their short time away. He would see to the ring very soon.

"Anything else?" he asked, somewhat expectantly.

"Yes, just the best man and the ushers. Maria's going to be my bridesmaid. Mummy's got the dress in hand."

Mike took out his diary. As he made scribblings he told Sable that his brother was happy to be best man and two cousins would be ushers. His parents had also booked the weekend.

"Good, well done, darling," she said as she ate another cream cake. Sable had told her mother that she would not be moving into the matrimonial home in Belgravia until they were back from honeymoon. Her parents fully agreed.

24

Some friends of Henry's, a charming gentleman with his equally charming wife from the City, were sitting in about the same place as before. They were in the church and bang on time. The big day had come. As they looked around them, Charles and Daphne Porter realised that they were in just about the same pew – when poor Sable had had that supremely embarrassing moment as she cross-examined Harold Jones.

As they carefully looked about them and discreetly observed others, they recognised some familiar faces on their side of the church, but not on the other. He was the new man. That whole side of the church would consist of new people. Charles and Daphne had been told a little bit about Mike and they just hoped he was of sound character. Having a house in Eaton Place was quite an eye-opener and they presumed it would become the matrimonial home. Lucky girl.

"But he's a property developer, darling," said Daphne as she whispered to her husband by way of a reminder. "I don't like them. Why couldn't she marry a solicitor like you and Henry?" Charles was at a slight loss for words. He moved his head and then his hands. "I bet he's a wide boy!" said Daphne.

In a whisper, Charles reminded his dear wife that she had not even met him. He was almost going to accuse her of being prejudiced but then thought better of it. After all, he reminded himself, he and his dear wife seldom argued. It was one of the hallmarks of their successful, long marriage.

She had not finished. "I just hope he wears morning clothes and a top hat."

Poor Charles. His wife had always been very critical of other people, especially if they demonstrated a lack of self-discipline and lack of style. "Of course he will," he chirped.

Daphne looked sternly at her husband. Charles knew that his wife had been brought up in a very strict household with an equally strict mother. From what he had gathered, he was convinced that there was some German blood somewhere, possibly on his mother-in-law's side. Somebody, somewhere had owned a house in Weimar in Central Germany, once home of the new democratic government after the First World War. The topic seldom came up in conversation now but it had done in earlier times. No wonder she was always going on about discipline, he thought. The Germans possessed far more than we did, or so she contended. But at least the British had a sense of humour.

Charles and Daphne watched Henry and Gloria come in and gave them a welcoming hug, as old friends do. Henry seemed ageless and Gloria was still full of curves and colour.

"The ushers are in morning clothes, darling," commented Charles.

Daphne examined them. "I would expect nothing less," said Daphne, in a tone which almost made Charles laugh. Luckily he stifled it. Charles and Daphne were so very pleased that Sable wore a totally new wedding dress for her marriage to Mike. Maria wore a new colour as well.

As the proceedings were about to start, Charles just wondered how many couples had actually analysed the meaning of the promises they were about to make. They observed the marriage and then had a thoroughly agreeable afternoon in the church hall, where the reception was held. There were a number of speeches but, thankfully, none too long. When it came, humour radiated from the best man's lips. He even had all the jokes and stories written down in a big red book. Daphne was most impressed. She leant across to her husband. "You see, organised and disciplined." Charles smiled at her. Yes, but was the bugger German, he asked himself.

After the speeches, sandwiches and champagne, Charles and Daphne waited with the other guests for the happy couple to appear in their going-away outfits. And very soon, they had all waved the car goodbye.

Gloria went up to Daphne. "Have you got time to come back to the house? We're having just a few friends round." Daphne gave Gloria a hug and hoped the future would be full of brightness. Charles just gave Henry a pat on the back and expressed the same sentiment.

***

The new Mrs Grantham wore a blue suit of skirt and jacket as her going away outfit. She wore black shoes and had a yellow scarf, with large blue dots, around her neck. Her husband admitted that his wife looked a picture. Mike wore a blue suit that had a check pattern to it. He too wore new black shoes.

Sitting on Sable's lap was the road atlas of Britain because she wanted to see where they were going. Soon Windsor Castle was on the right side of the car. "Find the road to Maidenhead. The hotel's on the right before the turn-off to Bray," he said as he glanced across.

Sable could then see it. The location seemed to have extensive grounds and a river frontage. For a moment, Sable reflected on the day. It had gone well. But she was sorry that neither May Ling nor Jill had been able to get over for it. It did not really surprise her as both would have had long journeys by air. Perhaps they might be able to come over to London in the future. She would be able to offer them hospitality in her new home, which she had yet to move into. Once she was at the hotel, she would make sure she sent an email to them both.

Soon Mike had swept into the car park of this very old-worldly hotel frontage. As they sat and admired the entrance, she could see that it had been built as a country house.

"Victorian and gothic and built in 1859 – I've even done my homework," said Mike proudly, "and it's even got gargoyles."

Once they were upstairs in their spacious room, they were able to appreciate the lovely view. Their room overlooked the garden with its extensive lawn sweeping down to the River Thames. There was also a large marquee, with people milling about. Perhaps there had been a wedding, thought Mike.

"I'm going to take a long bath. Is that all right, Mike?"

"Fine. I'll go downstairs and see if there's a business centre."

There were a few computer terminals, which he might use later on. Right now he had plans to visit the marquee and see what was going on. He liked hunting – a characteristic of which Sable had no knowledge. It turned out to be a big birthday party, so Mike put on his big smile and gatecrashed. As he was chatting to a youngster, who assumed Mike was a guest, he noticed a pretty Asian waitress dressed in black. All the staff wore black.

He later eased himself away and moved closer to the girl. He got into conversation with her and asked her where she lived. As she filled his glass, he got as close to her as he could and told her how wonderful she looked. He managed a gentle pat on her bottom, and had they been completely alone, he was going to slip his hand into the vent of her skirt. He gave her a full smile and told her he wanted to see her later on and have her phone number. She returned a smile and said she had to keep on with her work. There were other guests to be attended to. She apologised.

Mike wanted to take her behind the marquee but realised there was precious little time. After finishing his drink, he returned to his room.

When Sable was hanging up her clothes, she examined a few of the labels on Mike's suits. She recognised the good quality and was impressed.

When they were nearing the end of their dinner she dropped a hint that they still had to consummate their marriage. She then whispered a few words.

"A good job I ate some steak," he said.

"So what's the plan for tomorrow, darling?" she asked eagerly.

He outlined their itinerary, which would start off with a journey on the river, with lunch on board. He also planned to take her to Windsor, explore Bray on foot, do some shopping in Maidenhead and see if there was any horse racing to watch.

Sable made sure that they were not too late to bed. She had bought a beautiful new little negligee which she hoped would set her husband's pulse racing. It did indeed, because at the height of his ecstasy, a paroxysm of passion poured into her pussy. It left them both tired out and they slept extremely well.

The journey on the river took them past one of the most famous restaurants in the country, the Fat Duck, some say even in the world. It was exceedingly difficult to get into at the best of times, apparently. Mike would not be taking her there. What Sable did enjoy was her walk round the village of Bray. She loved the tiny village with its flint, brick and half-timbered cottages strung along the Thames. While she spent time admiring the almshouses, Mike inspected the war memorial made of distinctive white limestone. There wasn't a village in England that had not been touched by the call to the Front in the First World War.

Two days later she sent an email to her mother, describing one or two events. The modern shopping centre in Maidenhead, with its mall, was well worth a visit as was their visit, to Windsor – always a pleasant pastime.

At the end of the honeymoon they were back in London. A small removal van had been booked for the weekend so that all Sable's effects and small items of furniture could be moved to her new home in Belgravia. Henry and Gloria had helped all they could. They had even provided a bottle of champagne and a large celebratory cake. By Sunday afternoon all Sable's effects were installed and she would then spend the next few days sorting things out. She wanted to give some of her old clothes to charity, anyway, they had seen better days.

The double bed was comfortable enough while their bathroom was very modern. The kitchen was also modern. Sable hoped they would also be able to entertain and make good use of the large dining table. She wanted to know if May Ling could also stay the odd night if and when she came to London. Mike said he would always be happy to see her.

Gradually Sable knew she would feel the house was hers – or at least, half hers. She also discovered that Mike liked to swim for twenty minutes before his evening meal.

***

"So it's Mrs Sable Sophie Grantham, then?" said her boss, Miles Copeland.

"Yes." Sable smiled at him. Sable placed a sheet of paper on his desk which gave her new name and new address.

"You'll need to give this to HR, IT, pensions and salary division. It's all a bit of a nightmare when a female member of staff gets married. Oh, and medical division as well," commented Miles. "Better to be safe than sorry. And in due course, HR will update your new passport with your new name." He looked down at the sheet of paper, then across at the map of London which had occupied a wall for a long time.

"Your journey to work – will it be easier now?"

Sable nodded, "I'm really not too far from Victoria. I can take the Underground or a bus."

He stood up. "I hope it all goes really well, Sable. If there's anything I can do, you can always come and see me."

Sable thanked him and left. She had much work to do and staff to talk to.

***

Mike's work had been going well, so he said. He had been away each day in various parts of the City where he was working on residential properties. The key to a good development was a damn good builder and in recent years he had been lucky. His latest builder was a man called Ricky and he was good. Mike always knew that the correct specifications would be used – unlike some crooked builders who tried to save money here and there and break the law at the same time. Ricky was reliable, and as far as Mike could tell, he was honest. And so Mike would not hesitate to recommend him to any business colleagues.

One day he told Sable he would be home late because he and Ricky were going to a business chum's house for a business party. Sable said she would cook for him if needed.

At the party Mike got to know some of the business girls and a couple of hostesses who were in charge of the catering. He often sensed good sexual chemistry and when he did, he made the most of it. He just loved to have girls sit on his lap so that he could tickle them and squeeze them. Some of the girls just loved it when he kissed them on the breast or tickled them up their skirts.

At the end of the party, when Mike got home, he was unaware that some of the girls' scent had rubbed off onto him. Sable noticed it when she put his suit away but said nothing.

A few days later, Mike finished a site visit earlier than expected. So he paid a visit to Shepherd Market before going home. He found himself introducing himself to Francine, who appeared to be the madame of the establishment. She was mature and very friendly and keen to help this new customer. After describing his preferences, Francine opened a large folder and showed Mike some glossy photographs. He swiftly made his decision and very soon he spent an hour with a small French girl. Her name was Julie. She was really quite petite but was full of excitement when she lay on top of him. With Mike on his back, they had satisfying sex in that position. Luckily, she stifled her screams when she had a climax. She asked him when he would be coming again, and he said probably quite soon. He was intrigued to see her wear a skimpy black thong under her miniskirt. So why did Sable so often favour formal panties, especially when she went to the Foreign Office? Was it regulation?

The fact that he had actually committed adultery did not cross his mind. As far as Mike was concerned, having sex with a tart, however nice she was, did not constitute adultery. You had to do that with a friend or business acquaintance. To Mike's way of thinking, a tart was like retail goods. You bought a service and that was it. If you liked the service, you could return and buy it again. It was like going to the supermarket.

But Julie excited him.

***

Sable was really keen to meet Hugh Mannston, the prime minister. Mike consulted his diary. "You could come with me next Saturday. I'm meeting him at nine."

And so it was that Sable had her chance to meet the prime minister as well as the much-talked-about bolt-hole that her husband was converting for him.

Hugh Mannston was young, slim, good-looking with dark brown hair. He was also a bachelor. He had blue eyes and a charming, polite personality. She had seen him on TV in the House of Commons on numerous occasions, especially when he had to defend the government's position at Prime Minister's Questions on Wednesdays. He came across as confident and unruffled.

Mike took Hugh and showed him some samples of slate, which he wanted him to choose. There were also a few technicalities concerning the conservatory which required a decision as well.

When Hugh discovered that Sable was in the Foreign Office and was training to be a diplomat, he was particularly interested. He made noises about her coming to the odd reception at Number 10, especially at his Christmas and summer parties. Sable told him that she was currently spending her time improving her new home in Eaton Place.

Only Mike suspected that Hugh had financed his bolt-hole by borrowing from a Russian friend of his, now living the life of an exile in England.

When there was a suitable pause in the conversation, and Hugh was getting ready to depart, Sable asked him a burning question. She wanted to know if he was acquainted with the Dutch PM.

"Gerit? Oh yes, actually I've met most of them at various summits. And I saw the French prime minister once but only socially. The president of France is my equivalent, not the French prime minister."

Sable thanked him graciously.

When Hugh got back into his car, he noted that she was distinctly charming and she also possessed an air of authority about her. He expected her to go far. He thought she would also make an excellent foreign secretary if she ever went into politics.

***

In Paris, Sable's dear friend, Henri, had been busy looking into who might be a successor to his father as prime minister. Roland Tassier had been an excellent PM and it was well known that the president had full confidence in him. But when Henri was reading one of the Parisian newspapers, he had read about another politician called Gustave Laurent. According to the press he was a bachelor and also popular in his part of France. He came over well on French television.

Henri sent a brief message to Sable in case she discovered that Gustave Laurent was on a visit to London. At least she would recognise the name. Sable sent best wishes to them all.

***

Every time Henry and Gloria visited Eaton Place, they could recognise that their daughter was putting her stamp on the place. It was new curtains and new colours here and there. And what a wonderful home it was. Mike was good in that he allowed Henry and Gloria to go round on occasional weekends to use the small swimming pool. Henry just loved it and Sable would always join them. Mike usually preferred to swim after work during the week.

Whilst everything was supposedly normal between Mike and Sable, he made a second visit to Shepherd Market after work one day. After being welcomed by the delightful Madame Francine, he soon found himself enjoying an hour in Julie's lovely company. She was very agile and keen to assume any position that Mike wanted to experience. He had to admit that he felt very relaxed with her and he put this down to chemistry. And he always gave Julie a passionate kiss when he left her. He paid by cash but in future he decided he would pay by card. Madame was most agreeable to do business with him.

That night, when Sable was hanging up his suit jacket, she noticed familiar scent on the material. It was not her perfume. She wondered if she ought to run this past her mother or should she try to sort it out herself. No, she would tackle it head-on.

BOOK THREE

25

Six months later it was very clear to Sable that something was badly wrong. She had done all she could as a loving wife to make the house an agreeable home for them both but Mike was clearly seeking comfort elsewhere and on a regular basis. She had no idea why but she was not prepared to put up with it. It demeaned her. First, she needed some sound advice. Sable chose a day and booked the appointment. It was in the City.

Informing her staff that she had to be out on business from two until four, she had made her way to the solicitors that had been recommended to her.

"Mrs Grantham, do you have proof of his sexual behaviour with this other person – a name, for example?"

Sable was sitting opposite the person who would, in due course, handle her divorce. Her name was Miss Frost and she was good at litigation. She was sharp and alert.

"No. Not yet. But I am sure I can obtain it," replied Sable.

Miss Frost was nodding. "If we can prove adultery then you have a straightforward case. If not, then we have to think of making a case of his 'unreasonable behaviour'. And indeed we might have to argue over it. But let me tell you something – do you remember those words 'for better or for worse', which you both uttered in the church in the presence of the congregation – in effect, witnesses?"

"Why, yes," said Sable.

The solicitor then went on to tell her about a fairly recent divorce case in the High Court which had come to set a precedent in divorce law. A lady petitioner had been separated from her husband and had been living on her own for over two years. The judge had examined her petition and had then asked the lady some questions. She explained that she was generally unhappy in the marriage and she just could not see the situation improving. The love had disappeared and there was no companionship at all. So they had been separated for two years.

The judge reminded her of the marriage contract that she had entered into, and the fact that she had made certain promises, regardless of the situation, whether it was good or bad. He explained to her that she had signed up to a life that would either be better or worse and that she had to accept the rigours of marriage, in effect, good days, bad days and unhappy days. He said that if life became worse in a marriage situation, then you had to accept it. In effect, when people get married, they enter a risk area. There were ups and downs in any marriage – you agreed to that.

He denied her a divorce and told her to go back home and remain there for another three years – she would then be entitled to a divorce under the five year separation rule.

"Interesting," admitted Sable, "but in my case I think proving adultery will be the answer."

"Well, if you can secure that information in due course, however painful that may be, then you will have a good case," said Miss Frost, with a cheery smile.

When Sable left the premises she returned straight to the Foreign Office; all was well at her desk. There were some minor things that needed her attention. She sat there thinking, not so much about her job but about how and when to confront her husband. Why did this have to happen to her? If he was home tonight, and not late, she would tackle him then.

***

She had decided to make a salad supper – that way things would be much easier in the event of a showdown. She sat in the dining-room, waiting.

When Mike returned, he seemed cheerful enough. He had come from the City, or so he said. Sable decided not to waste time. "Mike, are you having sex with someone?"

The words caught him completely offguard. He turned a red colour. "What do you mean, darling?" He tried to laugh it off.

"Are you having fairly regular sex with a tart, not too far from here?" Mike was at a loss to give a coherent answer. What had happened? "Mike, what is her name? This tart. What is her name?" demanded Sable. "Her scent has been all over your suit jackets. And it's not your secretary, either. This is a French perfume!"

Silly words tumbled out of his mouth. "Of course not, darling. Why would I?"

Sable retorted quickly, "Yes, Mike, why would you, after all that I can give you. Answer me that?" He sat there, somewhat speechless. "What's her name, Mike? This piece of shit?"

That did it. Nobody was going to call her a piece of shit. "She's not a piece of shit!" He then realised he had given it all away; he had walked into her trap.

She kept the pressure on. "What's her name, Mike?"

He looked despondent, caught out, like a trapped animal, with no place to hide. "Her name is Julie. I only went there after a bad day at the building site," he mumbled.

She looked at him, with her face full of venom. "And when you lay between her legs, was that your little oasis of contentment?" He had no reply for there was guilt written all over his face. "And from where does she operate, this tart?" asked Sable, firing another broadside.

He looked around the room. He then mumbled, "Shepherd Market."

"That old haunt. I might have known it," she said. "Right, I have a list of demands, Mike. First of all, write down her full name on this piece of paper. It'll be a lot simpler if you cooperate, otherwise I'll have to use a private investigator." She pushed pen and paper over to him.

As he scribbled her name, she told him what she wanted. He would have to vacate the house inside a fortnight and live elsewhere, give her his new address, start leading his own life in his new dwelling, prepare for forthcoming divorce proceedings on the basis of his adultery; the little tart would be named as co-respondent.

"And after all that I could have offered you over the years, you broke those very important promises - with what, a little French tart! You're a bloody fool, Mike. And what could she offer you that I can't? No, don't even attempt to answer that; it'll be dirty and sordid." Sable almost bellowed the last few words at him.

Mike sat there, wounded yet angry. He thought he had kept it all so secret, his dear little Julie – the French tart that Sable referred to.

"You'll sleep in another room until you have moved out. A lettings agent will find you a flat. You've ruined things, Mike. A bloody fool. Give me that piece of paper. Is the address on it?"

"Yes," he said, only just audibly. He pushed it over to her.

Sable read the name of the little tart – a Mademoiselle Julie Landre. The confrontation over, Sable disappeared into the kitchen to finish her salad. At least she had obtained some of the vital information that her solicitor would require. And he had admitted it.

Having completely lost his appetite, Mike went upstairs to move some things out of the main bedroom and into one of the spares.

Next morning, she waited until Mike had gone to work. She would telephone her parents, then later on, Maria. She would try to see her parents at the weekend as she also was in need of much support. The shock and the truth were real enough.

***

At the weekend her mother wanted Sable to release all the emotion, the tension and anger and just let it all come flooding out. But for some reason it did not happen. Her daughter remained in a sort of businesslike mood, perhaps because she knew things had to be done and she was the only person to see it all through. A lesser mortal might not have behaved like that. Gloria and Henry wer impressed with their daughter's stoical behaviour.

At her parent's request, Maria came round as well, in order to give support to her best friend.

Looking to the future, Henry wondered about the house in Eaton Place. "And you want to keep it?"

296

Sable knew what she wanted. She had done much to transform it from a bachelor house into a matrimonial home. "I'm going to keep it," she said defiantly. "It's half mine."

Henry knew it might not be that simple. "Well, darling, the solicitors will doubtless argue over it in the settlement. You might have to pay him something. Anyway, that's a long way off. Keep up your strength, darling, we'll be behind you all the way."

One evening, Maria had popped round to generally help Sable sort a few things out in Eaton Place. She also had a swim. As they sat chatting, Sable had an idea.

"You know, darling, I need a live-in housekeeper. I need someone to prepare meals for me when I come home late from the office, do the shopping, and generally look after the place, especially if I go overseas again."

"A good idea," agreed Maria, "so why not advertise?"

Sable looked at her. "Good thinking, darling. I will."

Sable knew it might take awhile, and there were other things to do, but she gradually put things in train. When she was in her bedroom and one of the drawers was open, she did something that she had clearly forgotten to do. With some difficulty she removed the two rings that had once sat happily on her left hand. Instead of throwing them in the waste bin, in a rage, she placed them in a small container and closed the drawer. One day she would have the engagement ring valued.

Two weeks later, Mike was installed in a flat, his new home. Sable had the address and decided to make a visit soon. She still regarded him as a total bastard for completely wrecking the marriage. What could Julie possibly offer him that I couldn't, she asked herself?

She chose a morning and just hoped he would not be there. She took a bag full of domestic items, including sellotape and sharp scissors. Once at the flat, she found the caretaker and carefully explained who she was. Would he be awfully kind and let her in as she had forgotten her husband's keys? There was no reply from the doorbell.

Naturally he obliged.

Once inside, she set to work. She found his wardrobe and pulled out four of his best suits. She smelt them – Julie's French scent was still detectable. Bastard. Moving over to the light, she took out her scissors and proceeded to hack into one of the jackets. She then ruined the lapels. With the second suit jacket, she added two extra vents in the back and then cut up the pockets. Moving onto the next jacket, she destroyed the inner pockets completely. And with the fourth suit, she cut out the bottom of all the pockets in both jacket and trousers. She also carefully ruined the hip pockets. She then hung all the suits back in the wardrobe as if they had never been moved.

Before she left, she rearranged the chairs in the simple dining room and then put the two chairs in the kitchen onto the table.

She decided not to leave a note. She also knew that he would change the front door locks as soon as he could. Her mission was done. "That, dear chap, is what I do to somebody who fucks a French tart and thinks I won't notice."

26

Mike had to hurry home because he was due to attend a party, sort of a business gathering in Pimlico. He was taking Julie, who was now becoming his girlfriend rather than his comfort-girl. He promised to pick her up at eight.

As he approached his flat the caretaker didn't say anything as he assumed all was well between him and his dear wife. Everything seemed to be normal. The caretaker was going into another flat to do some maintenance work.

Once inside, Mike took a few paces forward before stopping. His heart missed a beat. He then saw that it was only the chairs that had been moved – perhaps the care-taker had been in. He put them back into their former positions.

He poured himself a drink and took out his phone in case it rang. He then prepared himself a quick sandwich in the kitchen as he did not know at what time they might be eating. Since Julie was slim and slight, he assumed she had only a modest appetite.

He then took a quick shower before dressing. He changed his shirt and tie and then had to decide on which suit to wear.

He pulled out one of the suits. The trousers fell to the floor and looked decidedly odd. He then inspected the jacket – and he saw Sable's handiwork. Mike sat down and shouted a whole string of obscenities. Hastily, he pulled out the other suits that were in the same row, and saw all the damage that had been done. He shouted yet again, so loudly that someone in the adjacent flat could just hear him. He sat on the edge of the bed – what else had she done?

There was no time to inspect his entire wardrobe. He had to get ready and get out to collect his little French girl.

He wore a blazer that, thankfully, had not come under Sable's knife. He walked to his car, cursing at every step. What a nasty bitchy thing to do – did he really deserve it? As he drove away, he made a mental note to speak to the caretaker and get the frontdoor locks changed as soon as possible.

Little Julie would never do a bitchy thing like that, surely?

***

Sable's solicitor had said that she was quite happy to receive messages and information by email so Sable told her about the confrontation with Mike. She gave the name and address of the French tart – the co-respondent, which Mike had divulged without much of a struggle. She also informed her of Mike's address at his flat.

She then received some good news. A person called Jane had answered her advertisement because she was looking for a position as a live-in housekeeper. Sable invited Maria to come round and help to give a joint interview. It transpired that Jane had just finished working for a film producer in Hampstead. The producer was emigrating to California so Jane was out of a job, preferring to remain in London.

Sable outlined her duties and was quick to point out that she was not able to match the salary that a film producer paid. Jane said she was just happy to have a job rather than join the dole queue.

"I hope you like Selfridges. I do quite a lot of shopping there," added Sable.

Jane's references and previous work experience were very acceptable. At the end of the interview, they said they would contact her very soon.

When Sable received a reply from her solicitor, she discovered it was entirely probable that she would have to make some sort of payment to Mike if she wanted to stay in the house. It was, after all, a large and expensive house that Mike had bought – and it had only served as the matrimonial home for a short time, albeit thanks to Mike's entirely reckless behaviour.

Sable then had a thought. She would invite Hugh Mannston to dinner, in his private capacity, and see what help or advice he might be able to give her. After all, had he not borrowed a huge sum of money to finance his bolt-hole in Belgravia from a likely Russian businessman? Thank goodness she had already met him and had got on well with him.

She sent a message to Maria, outlining her plan to invite the PM and wondered which day of the week, and which week, would suit him. She planned to send a letter of invitation, partly handwritten, to Hugh Mannston Esq, to Number 10.

Maria said her diary was fairly empty; she also told Sable that this dinner would be a good test of Jane's skills.

When his private secretary gave him the letter, Hugh was touched that the invitation had come from Sable Grantham. Unusually, it was also inviting him to select the date, because of his very heavy schedule – weekend or weekday, it was up to Hugh and his secretary to choose.

***

Hugh's secretary responded, giving a preferred date, saying that Hugh would be delighted to come.

"I'll talk to my Russian friend and ask him to make contact with you, shall I?" ventured Hugh as he smiled at Sable at the dining table.

"That would be wonderful, Hugh." Sable opened her handbag and gave Hugh her business card. "He can contact me either at the Foreign Office by email or here, whichever is most convenient for him. He must be a busy man."

Sable was overjoyed that Hugh was so willing to help. Maria thought it was a major coup. The prime minister, in his private capacity, was guest of honour at the dinner party in Eaton Place. His staff were seated in the kitchen, where Jane was looking after them. His car was in the underground car park, as was the police escort motorbike. The date had been arranged by his personal secretary at Number 10.

Henry and Gloria were also present, partly because Henry's firm had done some private work for Hugh. Henry had liked Hugh enormously. The man was good-looking and straightforward. It had been a pleasure doing business for him.

Hugh drank a little more wine. "Oh, I wish every evening in government could be like this. You know, there are two things which are really trying – one of them is Prime Minister's Questions and the other is entering into negotiations with the French."

Gloria just could not help but giggle. Henry did his best to quieten her.

The PM continued, "Luckily, our foreign secretary and his team do most of the talking with the French. I do really very little except when it's a summit and I have to converse with the president."

Sable just had to ask. "Hugh, have you spoken to the new man yet – he's very young?"

Hugh looked at Sable with a smile. "I did speak very briefly with him on the telephone soon after he was confirmed as the new president." Hugh then made an aside. "His wife is most charming but she still puzzles me."

"Yes, there is a bit of an age difference," said Henry softly.

"But it's no impediment," chirped Gloria happily.

"Well, that's right," agreed Hugh. "It does seem to work."

"Long may it continue," added Sable.

Sable and Hugh made frequent eye contact and seemed happy to do so. Hugh was clearly sorry that Mike and Sable had split up after such a very short time, but it happened. It was now obvious to him why she wanted to keep the house, which she had turned into a matrimonial home. To keep it she would have to pay Mike a lot of money, or so he assumed. Hence the need for her to borrow from a source other than from a bank.

When Hugh departed, everyone wished him well. He had special thanks for Sable, both as hostess and as a new friend. He said he looked forward to seeing her again. He gave her a gentle kiss before leaving the house.

The car had been brought up and Hugh was soon on his way back to Downing Street. The other guests also departed. Actually, they had all had the time of their lives.

Sable and Maria sat back in armchairs and reflected on the evening. Dare they call it a triumph? It had been simple yet so happy and successful.

"Darling, well done," said Maria. "That's one to write home about, I think."

Sable had been mesmerised by Hugh. She didn't think she would sleep that night.

***

Henry and Gloria had noticed the very friendly interaction between the prime minister and their daughter, single again but, of course, technically, still married. They wondered what opportunities they might have to see each other.

A few days later, Henry was reading *The Daily Telegraph* . On one of the inside pages something caught his eye. It was under 'forthcoming marriages' that he read of the announcement of the engagement between Mr Harold Jones and Miss Sofia Danovich of Budapest. Mr Jones's address was simply given as London.

He called Gloria.

She read with interest. "That must be Harry," she said. She then sat, thinking about it. "I think we'll keep that quiet, shall we?"

27

Sable's house in Eaton Place had a courtyard garden that she decided would lend itself well to a post-divorce summer party. She thought an eleven forty-five start would be good. She chose a Friday and hoped it would suit everyone.

Sable realised that it would have to be when Parliament was in summer recess. She would want Hugh to be present as the principal guest.

Her solicitor had been brilliant. Equipped with very good negotiating skills, Miss Frost had negotiated a settlement with the other side. In order for Sable to keep the house, she had had to pay a sizeable sum of money over to Mike. To do this, Sable had been lucky enough to find a sympathetic ear in the Russian friend of Hugh Mannston. He had been only too happy to help her and lend her the money.

And so a get-together of dear friends was called for. Maria helped Sable organise the guest list. Once they had some idea of numbers to invite, it was a question of who could actually make it. Jane would turn her talents to the catering. Maria would supervise.

Once the date had been set, she sent emails out to May Ling and Jill Kamudona to see whether they could come to England. She sent a personal paper invitation to Hugh Mannston at Number 10, and an email to the Dutch PM. To the Dutch PM, she recommended that he fly British Airways from Amsterdam to Heathrow Terminal 5. Sable wasn't very concerned whether he came or not. If he did come, he could always chat to his British counterpart.

She would like to have invited Henri but did not feel this was the right sort of forum; there would be other opportunities, she told herself.

Miss Frost said she would not miss the party for the world. Sable was unsure whether to invite her boss, Miles Copeland. She was unsure how he would get on with all the politicians, if they all turned up. Maria wondered if he would feel that he was being upstaged. Perhaps, best not to invite him.

***

When Hugh Mannston received his invitation, he conferred with his personal secretary and gave her some specific instructions. Two of them would be flying and they would stay at a hotel over the weekend and return on Monday morning. Please arrange everything with Flight.

The short holiday was to be a surprise. His security detail would of course accompany him when they departed from the address in Belgravia.

***

The party turned out to be a great success. It was an opportunity for Sable to relax and slightly let her hair down. Nearly everyone had arrived and Hugh was well on time. May Ling and Jill also made it and one of the first things they did was to have a photoshoot with Sable. It was such good fun to be together again.

May Ling and Hugh had a long conversation about the state of the economy in Hong Kong. At the end of it all, Hugh declared that the first-hand information that he had gleaned from May Ling was worth ten visits to the island. "The Chinese hide the truth from everyone and tell you what they want you to hear," declared Hugh. He just could not thank May Ling enough.

Jill managed to tell Hugh all about the woes in her part of West Africa – the poverty, the poor infrastructure, lack of clean water and near civil war in places. Hugh said he would bring it up in cabinet again and see what else could be done. He thanked her for her kind contribution.

Sable's Russian benefactor had been invited but, sadly, he had another engagement on that day. Busy man.

Sable was pleased to see that Hugh and Maria got on well. In fact, Hugh appeared to get on well with everyone, even the immediate neighbours whom Sable had also invited. She hardly knew them but they fitted in well.

The security detail were in the background and were forever present but again hardly noticeable.

Sable thought she was spending the weekend in London after the party, but Maria had been told otherwise. It was Maria who had packed one of Sable's suitcases and who had made sure her passport was nearby. She also knew they were returning either on the Sunday night or early on the Monday. After all, wasn't someone expected at the Foreign Office for a normal day's work?

Jane had cooked wonderful food. There was curry, salads, cold meats, beef casserole, rice, quiche and a large selection of cheeses with celery. May Ling and Jill were almost overwhelmed.

By two thirty, one or two people had departed, having greatly enjoyed themselves. Hugh told Maria that they ought to be departing by three. So could she organise Sable? No problem.

It was Maria's job to look after May Ling and Jill as they had been booked in to stay the night. In effect, Maria and Jane would handle things in Sable's absence.

***

Ever reliable, Jane was up early to make sure that Sable ate some breakfast before going on her adventure. It was almost the highlight of her life.

Sable found herself sitting in a smart Jaguar and the passenger beside her was the prime minister no less.

310

They were being driven through London, complete with police escort. Hugh did his best to convince Sable that he was doing his best to stay in a personal capacity but in reality it was hard not to wear just the one cap. He told Sable that his attendance at her lovely party was him in his personal capacity but once he was on the move, such as now, it was hard not to remain official. After all, supposing a crisis developed around the next corner?

Sable realised how difficult it was not to just be Mr Hugh Mannston MP.

As they chatted, she tried to watch where they were going. As if reading her thoughts, he said, "We'll soon be at RAF Northolt."

"Oh – really?" She was surprised. The police escort did wonders – traffic moved out of the way for them at every turning. "Is the car behind one of ours? I mean, yours?"

Hugh looked back. "Yes. Security and staff. My office."

Sable was most impressed. "I like the car."

"Yes. It's pretty good. If you put your foot down, you can do about one hundred and twenty, or thereabouts –pray to God it never happens."

Once they reached the airbase, there was a cursory search at the perimeter, with lots of RAF staff using walkie-talkies and mobile phones. Then, with minimum fuss, their car virtually drove right up to their aircraft.

"Just follow me, Sable. All our bags will be taken care of, I promise." He chuckled. "Nothing gets sent to the wrong place."

She followed him out of the car and up to the waiting steps of the plane. They were greeted by officers who saluted the prime minister and smiled warmly at her. Like an obedient servant, Sable followed Hugh down into the plane. They were led forward by RAF staff who were clearly used to this sort of thing. In no time at all, Hugh ushered Sable into a seat and he sat down beside her.

He looked at her warmly. "There, not too painful."

Instead of waiting endlessly for other passengers, all that had to be done was bring on their luggage and the prime minister's security luggage plus his staff. In a matter of minutes, the doors were closed and the engines became very audible. Not wishing to sound silly, she almost whispered to him, "Hugh, where are you taking me?"

"Don't you know?" She looked at him, puzzled but happy. Before he could give her a rational answer, they had to obey the seatbelt signs and sit upright. He whispered to her, "I'll tell you in a moment, my dear."

For the next five minutes she watched out of the window as London began to be left behind her. The jet climbed and gently banked as the pilots set a course for a southerly destination.

Soon she was conscious of a very smartly dressed steward standing in front of them both. He was offering them a drink. Sable chose a glass of white wine, while Hugh chose red. The drink came in seconds, complete with a huge tray of small biscuits and nuts. Sable just loved the array of nuts. This was something to tell Jane about when she got home. The plane was now on its course, heading south.

Hugh toasted Sable and thanked her again for such a splendid party at her house. They smiled warmly at each other.

"Well, we are heading in a southerly direction. Actually to a place that I have only been to once, albeit quite briefly. This time it will be so much better. Have you heard of the expression 'finding yourself between a rock and a hard place'? "

"Er – yes."

"Well, that's the clue."

She smiled. "Oh Hugh, you're talking in riddles. Is that how you talk to the Cabinet?" she said it with a big smile.

He was quick to respond, "No. That's how they talk to me!" They both laughed heartily, so much so that she nearly dropped her wine. She sensibly put the glass down. He sort of mumbled, "But if you do talk in riddles, nothing ever gets done." She laughed again. "Here's another clue: it's been a secure Royal Naval base in the Western Med for many a year. We've relied on it so many times."

She cracked it. "It's the Rock! It has to be Gibraltar."

He smiled at her. "Dead right. I think you'll like it. It's fun and very British. We stay at a hotel. You'll be well looked after. And I'll show you round the peninsular tomorrow, so long as you don't mind company." She looked slightly perplexed. "As prime minister, especially overseas, I can never be quite alone – security."

"I'll be right beside you, Hugh, and we'll be together." She meant every word of it.

After drinks, they enjoyed a very pleasant dinner and chatted amiably as the plane made its way towards southern Spain.

As they approached the Rock, Sable could see that the landing strip ran across the peninsular from west to east, from the Atlantic on one shore and to the Mediterranean on the other.

Then, with minimum fuss, Hugh and Sable left the aircraft and a car soon took them to their hotel, The Rock Hotel. As they stood briefly in the entrance hall, Hugh remarked that the hotel had been built in 1932 by the Marquis of Bute.

"It's a colonial style hotel," he said, with some pride.

Sable stared at the marble. "Wonderful."

After checking in, they soon found their rooms. Hugh made a note of where his personal detective was sleeping and then said he would call for Sable for breakfast at nine. With a need to maintain privacy, the hotel allocated a private dining area to these private guests from London. The hotel had done it before.

After breakfast, Hugh took Sable outside and showed her that the hotel was literally located at the base of the Rock of Gibraltar itself. It was quite a sight, so Sable took some photographs. Later during the day, and after conferring with his security detail, he took Sable to the Bristol Hotel for a drink.

"As a British Overseas Territory it's not bad at all," remarked Hugh. "But small."

"And do the Spanish still want it?" she asked.

Hugh was emphatic. "It's not negotiable. The sovereignty of this piece of land is not for discussion. That's how the residents want it."

Sable nodded her full agreement. "And quite rightly so. And even wearing my Foreign Office hat, I totally agree with you."

"It's also of strategic importance that we keep a Naval base here. You never know what's going to blow up in the future," he said.

Hugh liked the beer so much that he ordered another one. "Good beer, that," he said. "By the way, let's have a swim back at the hotel soon. Do you have a costume, Sable?"

"Yes I found it, thanks to Maria. She's very efficient. She found it in my house and packed it."

"Clever girl. "

After the swimming in the lovely sea, walking up into the Rock to appreciate the majestic panoramic

315

views and exploring some of the older buildings, the weekend soon turned into a wonderful memory.

When discussing when to return, Hugh said he could happily return quite early on Monday so that Sable would not be too late at her desk. It was agreed, so Hugh gave immediate instructions to his secretary and to the security detail.

The flight back to London was calm and happy. She and Hugh chatted about a range of subjects, not least of which was progress on his Belgravia 'bolt-hole'. He explained that Mike was getting on with chasing things up.

Sable then wondered about the future.

"We'll keep in touch, won't we, Hugh?" she said, possibly with a hint of concern.

He took her hand and held it firmly and kissed it. "Absolutely. I promise. I'm not going to let you disappear. You must come to dinner at Number 10 very soon. Will you do that, Sable?"

She smiled at him. "I'll be overjoyed to. And thank you for a simply wonderful weekend." She leant across and kissed him.

Once back at RAF Northolt, the familiar Jaguar car, complete with escort, made its way back into Central London. In no time at all they were driving down Whitehall, so Hugh gave orders for Sable to be dropped at the Foreign Office.

As Sable said her goodbyes, a member of staff took her luggage out of the boot. All she then had to do was pull her suitcase in the direction of her office.

She turned and waved at Hugh as the Jaguar turned round and made for Downing Street. She saw Hugh smile and wave back. Thank goodness, she thought. As she made her way back to the Foreign Office she could hardly believe that she had been away with the prime minister of the United Kingdom.

Not many girls could say that.